Schlock! Monthly

Editor: Gavin Chappell

This month's cover is GDFreak9 by  *Mike Knowles.*
Graphic design © by Gavin Chappell, logo design ©
by C Priest Brumley.

SCHLOCK! WEBZINE

Welcome to Schlock! the webzine for science fiction, fantasy, and horror.

Vol. 16, Issue 16
May 2021

Schlock! is a monthly webzine dedicated to short stories, flash fiction, serialised novels, and novellas, within the genres of science fiction, fantasy, and horror. We publish new and old works of pulp sword and sorcery, urban fantasy, dark fantasy, and gothic horror. If you want to read quality works of new pulp fantasy, science fiction or horror, Schlock! is the webzine for you!

For details of previous editions, please go to the website. Schlock! Webzine is always willing to consider new science fiction, fantasy and horror short stories, serials, graphic novels and comic strips, reviews and art. Submit fiction, articles, art, or links to your own site to editor@schlock.co.uk. We no longer review published and self-published novels directly, although we are willing to accept reviews from other writers. Any other enquiries also to editor@schlock.co.uk

ISBN: 9798745187773

EDITORIAL

In this month's edition we are featuring the disturbingly avantgarde horror art of Mike Knowles, renowned comic book artist of yore, whose work graced the pages of popular UK comics such as *Commando, Warlord, The Victor,* and *Starblazer.*

A story of sinisterly sorcerous forests is followed by political shenanigans down Picklock Lane. Claire meets the Tick Tock Man. Pain proves to be beauty. Neptune rises. Society collapses. Bold venturers set out. Two warriors seek out the Scorvyrn. And a group of aviators encounter aerial horror out of antiquity.

We have news of Liz Butcher's latest novel, *Never Never,* and Darren Ward's new gorefest, *Beyond Fury.* And in a final vignette, eighty year old Euphemia proves to be tougher than she looks.

—*Gavin Chappell*

IT CAME FROM INSIDE THE INKWELL! By Vincent Davis

"WORST CASE OF RESTLESS LEG SYNDROME I'VE EVER ENCOUNTERED!"

Vincent is an artist who has consistently been on assignment in the art world for over twenty years. Throughout his career he has acquired a toolbox of diverse skills (from freehand drawing to digital design, t shirt designer to muralist). His styles range from the wildly abstract to pulp style comics. In 2013, his work in END TIMES won an award in the Best Horror Anthology category for that year. When Vincent is not at his drawing board, he can be found in the classroom teaching cartooning and illustration to his students at Westchester Community College in Valhalla NY. He lives in Mamaroneck NY with his wife Jennie and dog Skip.

www.vindavisdesigns.com

VEX FOREST THREATENS BRISTOL CREEK ONCE MORE by Surina Venkat

An innocuous game of "truth or dare" played last Sunday left two teenagers dead and one hospitalized for the foreseeable future. Though the news did not cause a stir when it broke on Monday, there is now reason for concern: It appears the harm done to the teenagers was caused by a Vex Forest shrub located in the backyard of a house in the middle of Bristol Creek.

Four teenagers at Bristol Creek High School (who will go by different names in this article to protect their privacy) gathered for a sleepover at one of their homes. They set up a tent in the house's backyard and played various board games before deciding to end the night with "truth or dare."

"It started off with stupid asks," Kara, one of the teenagers, said. "Like daring each other to use conjuring spells and spilling our deepest secrets. I guess that's why I ended up daring [Robert] to kiss someone." Except when daring Robert to kiss the "hottest person in the tent," Kara "tried to be funny" and used the unfortunate terminology "suck face."

"He leaned over to [Allison] and began kissing her and their faces started sliding into each other's mouths," Kara said. "It—the nose and everything—went first and the lips went last. Robert was crying until his eyes disappeared."

According to Artie's parents, by the time they got to the tent Robert and Allison were faceless and convulsing. They went limp roughly five minutes later. When the paramedics arrived, the two teenagers were pronounced dead on the spot.

"It was irreversible damage," Lara Sanchez, one of the on-site mediwitches, said. "We knew from the moment we got there it had to be nature related."

Because of this, the paramedics did not attempt to resurrect Robert or Allison, which caused Artie to grow angry. He began screaming at them at a high enough volume to disturb the giant in the sewers, which caused several septic tanks around town to explode. And when the paramedics attempted to explain to him why his friends were dead, Artie began to scream out threats.

"I'll kill you," he reportedly shouted. "All of you, unless you get them back!" Artie then conjured a knife and attempted to stab the closest paramedic.

The paramedics managed to restrain Artie with rope and attempted to calm him with spells, but he continued to repeatedly attack them on the way to the hospital, causing them to suspect it was not just the boy's violent tendencies at fault. Once they reviewed the behaviour leading up to his initial attack and heard Kara's account of what had happened during the game, the paramedics determined that Vex Forest was involved. Sure enough, they discovered a Vex Forest shrub in Artie's house's backyard Monday morning. They were able to identify the plant as belonging to Vex Forest using a magical spell developed in the 1300s for the exact purpose.

Vex Forest has surrounded Bristol Creek since before the first human wandered into town, meaning it has likely existed long before the first homo sapiens, historians speculate. It has terrorized the town for centuries because being in close proximity with its plants gives organisms some of its immeasurable magic, which takes human speech and transforms it into reality.

Since Artie wished to kill the paramedics, the plant in his backyard instilled in him the determination and ability to do so. And since nature related magic is irreversible, Artie's desire to kill them has become permanent. To prevent Artie from fulfilling this desire, the hospital has thrown him in one of their holding cells, where he will remain until either the paramedics die or he does.

The magic of Vex Forest doesn't just work on humans—it works for magical and non-magical beings as well. Centuries ago, when the forest's plants grew all over town without consistent culling—historians speculate culling began in the 1400s, but can't be sure as records were burned—a couple turned into a pile of bird food, which their parakeet was found feasting on when their friends arrived to check on them. It wasn't until the parakeet's fourth family—the next door neighbours—met the same fate that authorities made the connection between a Vex Forest sprout in the neighbours' yard and the parakeet's murderous chirps.

Vex Forest also transforms writing into reality, discovered in the second year of 1931 when one year old Emilia Abbott began speaking in perfect sentences with a Russian accent, learned sambo overnight, and her body parts turned into fruits and vegetables over the course of the following year. The reason behind her transformation was revealed to be Bernard White, a school teacher with a Vex Forest plant on his windowsill. White had started writing a novel about an American spy and his love interest Emilia, a rival Soviet Union agent, whom he described as having "perfectly cherry lips," "breasts like watermelons" and "thighs as smooth and voluptuous as eggplants." Vex Forest does not take context into account, so when White wrote of his character Emilia having these qualities, the forest made them reality for the only Emilia within its reach: infant Abbott.

The forest's disregard for boundaries, context, and intent has led to some Bristol Creek residents calling it a "serial rapist," despite protests from those who believe the label is a misnomer. However, regardless of what you call it, the townspeople unanimously agree that Vex Forest is dangerous.

Justin Choi, a member of the Bristol Creek Community Service's (BCCS) Vex Border Guard, has patrolled the edges of the forest for fifty years to stop creatures from entering it. The forest is a popular tool for murderers and criminals because so long as they state their desired crime there, it will get carried out and there will be no evidence that implicates them. Due to the efforts of Choi and other Guard members, crimes committed via the forest have drastically dropped. Yet his patrols had Choi noticing the forest creeping towards the town's border walls, even though the forest tried to "be a sly b—stard about it."

"Its edge changes every year," Choi said. "Sometimes it moves five inches forward, sometimes it goes ten inches back and sometimes the changes happen in the blink of an eye. But it's kept moving forward overall. It used to be thirty feet away from the wall and now it's only five. It wants to take over the town and it isn't going to stop until it does."

The township tried to establish boundaries with the forest in the past through the use of controlled burning, but the forest retaliated by releasing large clouds of spores and seeds that spread all over town. The rest of 1945 saw Bristol Creek residents hunting the new born plants with shears and severed tongues, until Marietta Wilds famously lost her temper and burned the entire town to the ground just so people didn't keep coming to look for shoots on her sacrificial grounds.

"A witch's sacrificial grounds are personal," she wrote in an email. "No one should get to see where she drains her life energy—that's a violation of privacy.

"I don't regret burning down the town," she continued. "But I do wish that I'd warned everyone beforehand. A lot of people, including me, forgot to take their tongues with them. They got lost in the fire, so we couldn't reattach them."

The beginning of 1946 brought a meeting between the newly homeless and humbled Mayor Tom Brennan and Vex Forest, from which a truce emerged: The forest would leave the town alone and, consequently, the humans would stop cutting down its plants.

But the forest seems to no longer be holding up their end of the bargain. Since Sunday revealed the presence of Vex Forest plants within our midst, the BCCS's Detox Department has found three more plants on town grounds—but not before they caused damage. A mother can't stop singing since her child demanded her to only sing, a shade accidentally killed himself, and an entire class of kindergarteners has permanently "shut up" after their teacher yelled the words at them. Although the last one might be for the best—children, as the teacher pointed out in his defence, have the habit of saying what they mean even if it's better that they don't. No one knows this better than Karen Rainer, who had a Vex Forest pine tree appear overnight on the grounds of her mansion in 1941.

"I found out I was pregnant again in the bathroom of the Silver Tooth," Rainer said. "Glamourous, right? But I was excited and we thought Jack would be too. He wasn't, though. He got so upset when he found out we were having another baby."

"He told us not to have the kid because he wanted to be an only child," she said. "I had a miscarriage the next day. God, there was so much blood. And at first I thought, 'Was it me? Was my body wrong? Did I kill my child?' But then my husband and I remembered our conversation with our boy and we got so suspicious about the timing. We thought he had been the one to kill her. So we called Child Services and had them pick him up. When we found out it wasn't his fault and it was the forest's, we tried to get him back. But by then, they'd already killed him."

To prevent situations like the Rainers' from happening again, Mayor Brennan recommended that everyone have their mouths glued shut, especially children. He said severing tongues was another option, but after the mass muteness that befell the town last time they did that, it was probably best to stick with glue.

"We're working hard to find and eradicate the Vex Forest plants among us," Brennan said to an empty town hall. "However, we anticipate that this process will take a week or a couple years depending on whether the fog time-travels us to the past again. Please be patient and stay calm at a safe distance from vegetation."

Until Brennan announces the Vex Forest plants have been removed from town, it is recommended the residents of Bristol Creek watch what they say and write at all times and not make wishes or use non denotative phrases. After all, as Brennan pointed out, oft—repeated phrases like "I could eat a whole hydra" or "f—k the bear" could result in potentially fatal situations, so it's best to avoid using them altogether.

If you know anyone who's likely to use this situation to try to harm or murder you, please call the BCCS's Mutilation and Murder Victim Department so they can review your community service record and decide whether or not to assist them. To those that complain this policy is discriminatory, the BCCS would like to remind you that any problems that arise because of your record would have been entirely avoidable if you had been able to forge signatures for community service hours.

LOVECRAFTIANA

THE MAGAZINE OF ELDRITCH HORROR

CTHULHU'S DAUGHTER

John B Rosenmann

PLUS
CTHULHUVIAN
POETRY AND
ART

THE DEAD CAN SAIL

Ryan Klopp

VOLUME SIX, ISSUE ONE   WALPURGISNACHT 2021

THE HUGE REMAINS by EW Farnsworth

The Cracked Bell pub had become the de facto headquarters for the Transparency Party. This was convenient for Sheriff Fatty Millhouse and the management and staff of the pub. Citizens visited throughout the days running up to the elections, and newshounds followed the primary candidates, including chiefly Sir Hudibras, the odds on favourite for the PM slot. Two tabloid writers or their spies were ever present—Crenshaw and Straight, and their competition for readers caused sensational headlines daily. Crenshaw had an inveterate hatred of tentacle creatures, whose menace was displayed on the front pages. Less fanciful because of his concern for facts, Straight's articles kept his colleague's dream ware in check.

Fatty was showing his girth as never before. He was on the brink of self division though this was known only to his physician, a woman whose background as a hybrid made her particularly attuned to his plight. He sat holding forth at the table at the back of the pub while he tended his perpetual pint. He had five lessons to expound like a quotidian enema in the feverish time. His round face sweated, and his eyes gyred with excitement when he launched his defence of the Transparency plank focused on political and economic equality across all genetic backgrounds. He had not foreseen that after the rain and concomitant flooding, as the waters receded, an enormous free roaming tentacle appeared on the greensward of the park not far below the octopus's garden where Fatty had played with the resident octopod in all weathers.

Fatty was distraught at the finding, but he could do nothing to prevent Crenshaw and Straight from embellishing the find with headlines like, "Monsters

Lurk in the Park" and "Proof Perfect: Tentacles Roam Among Us!" As the sheriff had been the primary investigator of the poor creature's demise, he had the specimen transported to his own physician where, as he suspected, the tentacle was found to still be alive. Under the cover of darkness, he and a few of his associates conveyed the beast to the waterfront and watched it sink gratefully into its natural habitat. Fatty shed a tear as his own tentacle released the tip of the monster's. When he returned to his lodging, he went into labour and fissioned. His doctor, who was attending at the time, announced that the newcomer's green complexion indicated it was in perfect health. As for Fatty, he was ready to return to the pub the next morning as if nothing untoward had happened.

"Sheriff," Sam Straight called out as he entered the Cracked Bell, "you are looking remarkably healthy and thin today. To what do you attribute your good health? Some among the citizenry had whispered you might have to step down on the eve of the election. I bet against the majority, and I shall be happy to collect my winnings."

Fatty shook his moon face. "I am as you see me. I admit, the electioneering had taken its toll. But I have fully recovered now. You can print that in tomorrow's papers though it will not be as titillating as your usual fare."

"Will you make a comment on the strange disappearance of the giant tentacle? I assume you know it has disappeared from the clinic where you took it."

"I have no comment. I hope it has returned to its habitation and now is recovering from the rude interruption of its existence."

Crenshaw had come to the table. "It has probably gone to some belfry or watchtower from which it will menace the general population. It should have been taken straightaway to the fish market to be sliced up and sold with the other seafood. It's eat or be eaten. See what my tabloid has to say about the matter tomorrow. I'm afraid you can't avoid responsibility for the creature's escape."

Fatty changed the subject to a round of drinks, compliments of the Transparency Party. A new pint before him, he started his pitch on equality, and Sir Hudibras and his dame entered the turmoil to take their seats across from the sheriff.

"Don't stand on ceremony for us, Fatty. By the bye, you are looking singularly well today. We had worried about you."

Dame Hudibras nodded and sipped her drink. "What's this we hear about the escape of the giant tentacle?"

"Madam, you are remarkably well informed. The creature seems to have dematerialized during the night. All I can say is I wish it and its kind well. Can we all drink to that sentiment?"

Sir Hudibras lifted his glass and drank if half empty. "What is your assessment of the political situation, Sheriff?"

"Sir, you are gaining on the opposing parties steadily. The only question is, will your numbers be sufficient on election day to win?"

"How good are the polls that give me a twenty point lead?" This query brought forth an audible guffaw from Crenshaw, who pretended to be laughing about an unrelated matter.

"Sir, polls can be bought. This is still a capitalist country."

Dame Hudibras' nose went into the air. "I surely hope we shall avoid any imputation of impropriety."

"Yes, well, of course. We would not think about trying to buy the election. I must admit, though, the offers I have received for backing down have been most generous. It seems we are eating several other parties' lunches, so to speak. If we should withdraw before election day, we could pocket a tidy sum while having made our points sufficiently well to have portions become part of our opposition parties' platforms—all except for the plank about the tentacle creatures, who still appear to be a stumbling block all around."

Fatty looked at his glass and asked the inevitable question. "Just how much have you been offered to stand down?"

Dame Hudibras answered, "He has been offered twenty million pounds in an offshore account of his choosing and ten thousand gold ounce coins."

Fatty whistled. "That is a tempting offer, but your integrity would be jeopardized by taking it. What are you going to do?"

Sir Hudibras stuck his chin out. "I shall not make any move that would jeopardize my reputation or my wife's future. It's not a matter of money, but principle. I formed the platform of the new party, and we now have fifteen percent of the voters on our side. Millions of others may still join us. I hardly care about the damage I am doing to the extant parties. Our messages are permeating the air waves. I have gone 'all in' as the Americans would phrase our position. So there." The waitress came with a pitcher to top off the pints.

"You are an honest bloke, Sir Hudibras. That's what I like about you. If I were in your place, I could not resist the gold."

Fatty gestured for the waitress to move to another table with her pitcher. "How did you receive word about the bribes, Sir?"

The MP drew an unsigned letter from his pocket and let Fatty read for himself.

After perusing the missive, Fatty said, "This is stuff and nonsense. I bet one of the more unscrupulous newshounds wrote it to see what you would do. Crenshaw, is this your scurrilous work? I see the purple of your prose in every line."

The hack writer blushed but did not deny the accusation. "Well, Sir Hudibras, is it yes, or no?"

Fatty stood above the reporter and placed his palm on the man's shoulder as if conducting an arrest.

"Please don't arrest me, Sheriff. I did not write the letter. You know I don't have the kind of money it alludes to. If I did, I would not be a scribbler scrounging out a daily living."

Fatty loosened his grip on the man's shoulder and sat back down behind his glass. "Whoever did write the letter will not have satisfaction. Sir Hudibras is incorruptible. Isn't that so, Dame Hudibras?"

"That's why I love him so, Sheriff. We may be poor as church mice, but we are honest to the bone."

Crenshaw's eyes went wide. "That's my headline for tomorrow: 'Honest to the Bone!'"

Fatty said, "You can print that without further elaboration. Yet as unvarnished truth, will your editors go along?"

"You have a point there. I will have to fight for anything that does not sell papers."

The assemblage milled through the public house until closing time that evening. Just before last call, the polling numbers came in at 22%, and the Hudibras couple departed happy. The last to leave was the sheriff, who was troubled by the unsigned letter. As the chief law enforcer of Picklock Lane, he felt duty bound to ferret out the truth.

All night, Fatty made the rounds of his snitches to inquire about the author of the letter. All indications were that a book maker named Giles Handby was behind the epistle as he had bet heavily on a rival competitor to Sir Hudibras. Therefore, the sheriff visited Handby last and conducted an intensive interview.

"Giles Handby, I will not apologize for awakening you before daylight, because of the gravity of the matter I have to discuss with you."

"Sheriff, I know my rights. You are trespassing, and I can sue you for more than you even thought you would earn in your lifetime."

"I understand your threat, and I shall raise your bid considerably. If you write a letter to a candidate for the PM position, you will go to jail for twenty years and face a fine as large as the judge adjudicates." He handed the bookie the unsigned letter so he could read it.

Handby read the letter and laughed out loud. "So you think I wrote the letter."

"That's right. And I know your motive—greed. You thought by responding favourably to the letter, Sir Hudibras would be subject to blackmail."

"All right, Sheriff. I'll play along with your charade. I'm guessing you are Sir Hudibras' proxy, and your answer for him is yes, you'll take the offered bribe."

"Get dressed, Mr. Handby, as we're going to see where the truth lies right now."

"So you're going to add kidnapping to unlawful entry, are you?"

"Just get dressed. I will not have it said I have done anything improper, and I suspect that is what you will say if we don't get the situation clarified this night."

It was not a long walk from the apartment of Giles Handby to the waterfront where Fatty had released the huge tentacle. The two men sat on a bench by the water for a while as if they were there to observe the sunrise. After a quarter of an hour, the sun peeked over the edge of the horizon. An enormous tentacle snapped around Mr. Handby, making flight impossible.

"Good Grief! Help. This monster is going to crush me."

"I think I can help you, Mr. Handby, but you must tell the truth. If you hesitate or lie, I will let the creature take you home to his underwater palace and feed you to its young."

As if the thing understood what Fatty was saying, it lifted the bookie's body and drew it slowly toward the water as the man shrieked so loud the gulls and curlews mocked his protestations.

"All right. I'll tell. I'll tell you everything. Just stop this tentacle from what it's doing."

Fatty held up his hand, and the creature stopped for a moment.

"You had better talk fast, or I'll let the creature take you below the surface."

Handby was now fully alert to the threat. "Crenshaw put me up to the trick. He made bets on the opposition to the Transparency Party just as I did. We planned to triple our investment within three days, maximum."

"And there was no money and no gold, really."

"There was nothing but the idea of bribery. If the PM showed any inclination to take the bribe, we had him in our clutches. So that's the whole story. Will you set me free now?"

"You are going to accompany me to my office at the back of the Cracked Bell to write a statement spelling out what you have just confessed. If you hesitate to write the statement or make any changes in your story, I shall bring you back here and let the monster take you deep."

Fatty gestured and the tentacle released the bookie. It rapidly retracted its suckers and slipped back beneath the water's surface.

Fatty watched the bookie write his statement as both ate scones with tea. Giles Handby was happy to sign his confession. Then Fatty told him he could go.

It was now daylight, and the usual crowd began to assemble. Crenshaw and Straight brought the sheriff copies of their respective morning tabloids.

Fatty invited the two to have crumpets and tea. While they ate, he told them the story of Giles Handby's confession.

Straight said, "Fatty, this time I think you're positively barking mad."

Crenshaw was looking guilty and halfway standing as if he had to go to the loo.

"Before you leave, Crenshaw, I would like to show you my bona fides." He showed Crenshaw only the familiar signature as he handed the letter to Straight. Crenshaw raced to the back hallway and into the loo.

"Do I have permission to print this confession?" Straight asked.

"As long as you print it tomorrow and you don't divulge your source, yes."

Sam Straight was off like a shot to his tabloid editor. Crenshaw came out of the loo looking wan and sickly. He too ran off to see his editor. Fatty ate the rest of the crumpets feeling accomplished.

Rumours on Picklock Lane flew faster than the tabloids' news cycle. Sir Hudibras showed up at noon to hear the full story from his sheriff, who warned the candidate that he would see a reckoning in the next day's yellow press.

Sir Hudibras and his dame arrived early with copies of the tabloids. The Transparency Party was now at 24% approval, but at the expense of the opposition parties. Crenshaw, it happened, had visited his friend Giles Handby, and the two were cooking up more lies.

They might have levelled accusations of all kinds except Handby's letter had pre-empted them.

Handby was on the brink of accusing the sheriff of extorting the confession, but the sheriff rose to his full height and put his broad hand on the bookie's shoulder. Unseen by Crenshaw, Fatty's tentacle had crept up Handby's neck and settled behind his ear. The man shuddered in terror and stood down, aware that he and the sheriff were a moment's decision.

GAVIN CHAPPELL
Sinbad
AND THE
GREAT
OLD ONES

TEN MORE MINUTES by Scott McGregor

At 7:30 AM, Claire awoke to her alarm clock, a rackety, insufferable sound.

She contemplated how long it'd take to get ready for her day. Fifteen minutes to shower, ten minutes to get dressed, five minutes to gather her belongings, a twenty minute drive, and arrive at work by 9:00 AM. The way she thought about it, she could afford to stay in bed a tad longer.

Just ten more minutes.

So, she hit the snooze button and returned to sleep.

In a black, endless space, Claire sat in a chair, bound by a hundred chains. Across from her stood a man with a clock for a head, dressed in a white tuxedo. On what she assumed was the man's face, the hour and minute hands spun rapid, ticking slowly. He kept his arms crossed, not moving a muscle.

"Hello, I am Tick Tock Man," he said.

"Where am I?" she screamed back. "What do you want with me?"

"You're asleep, and you're here to feed me, so to speak. Ten minutes out there is ten hours in here. And every minute in here, you grow weaker as I absorb your essence."

"Then the second I wake up, I'll be free from here."

"Do you undermine my capabilities? Time can be rewound, if you know how to use it. Tell me, how many hours does the average person live for? How many times can I roll back the clocks until you're gone?"

And then, Claire began to weaken. She didn't know how or what, but it felt like something from within her was being sucked away.

Tick. Tock. Tick. Tock.

Nearly ten hours passed, and Claire could hardly breath, muscles stiff and eyes heavy. Then, a loud, thunderous ring entered the crevices of her mind.

"Time to wake up, Claire," Tick Tock Man whispered. "And, time to rewind the clocks."

At 7:30 AM, Claire awoke to her alarm clock, a rackety, insufferable sound.

She pondered how long it'd take to get ready for her day. The way she thought about it, she could afford to stay in bed a tad longer.

Just ten more minutes.

She hit the snooze button and returned to sleep.

Within the void, she felt her life force sucked from her, trapped as Tick Tock Man absorbed her essence. For hours, he stood perfectly still, and though he lacked eyes, she knew he watched her the whole time. A point reached where she grew too weak to move. To flinch. To even speak. She wondered what she might look like after he was finished with her. Perhaps a haggard, shrill carcass, forever asleep for ten minutes, trapped in time.

Tick. Tock. Tick. Tock.

Again, she heard the boisterous ring creep into her mind. She wished she could speak to herself the moment she awoke, pleading for one thing. Don't go back to sleep!

Then, Tick Tock man whispered, "Time to rewind the clocks, Claire."

At 7:30 AM, Claire awoke to her alarm clock, a rackety, insufferable sound.

Just ten more minutes.

She hit the snooze button and returned to sleep.

DEEP SPACE
DOGFIGHTS
DEATH FROM ABOVE

EYE OF THE BEHOLDER by Lorna Wood

It was hard to compete with her. She was tan, with beautifully cascading curls; I was ghostly pale, with stringy, straight hair. She had a dazzling smile; I had a gap toothed grin. She had gorgeous, bejewelled dresses with poofy skirts; I had faded jeans. She had delicate slippers; I had muddy sneakers.

She had all the gestures, too once I taught them to her the ones that make men and pageant judges take note. The stately pacing and turning, arms alternately held out over the skirt and brought up to convey heartfelt vanity and air kisses to the multitudes. The flirty hip jiggles and twerks to twitch the skirt. The lips poofed out (like the skirt), always with the waxed brows slightly raised, sometimes with an index finger or two pressed against the cheek. I never figured that one out, no matter how many times I watched her do it. Was it saying, "I'm kissable," or "I'm so stupid I just don't know what to make of it all"?

Of course, she would have been nowhere without me. I was the one who made sure she hit her marks, stopping for twirls exactly on the X's taped to the floor. I not only taught her the regular moves; I showed her how to tap dance for the talent segment. I was always the brains behind her success.

But that was small consolation when she posed for pictures after a long pageant day, with the lights glinting off her tiara, her canned smile brilliant against her bronzed skin. Inevitably, I was the one lugging the rollaboard, the goody bag, and the trophy to the car while Mom socked away the cash and told her how proud she was of her star daughter. Like the shooting star she was, she just shot off to freedom until next time.

She never grew up. Never had to. Eventually her childish charms wore thin on me, and even Mom. I tried to leave her and the whole mess of my childhood behind, but I still always had a sinking feeling that I just wasn't glamorous enough.

I think that's why, a few weeks after my long-time boyfriend left me for someone younger and prettier, I reached out to her for help. To my surprise, she had her own problems. I'd expected to pick her up where we left off, with her twirling through life, relying on gentlemen callers to pick up the pieces from the messes she made, but she seemed faint and weak, and spoke in a little girl whisper, like a moribund Marilyn Monroe. At first she just told me to take care of myself, by which she meant take long baths, drink tea, and binge watch the latest streaming series. I'm a teacher, and it was summertime, so I could follow her directions, but I found myself wallowing more and more in self-pity.

She didn't give up on me, though. On the contrary, she seemed to draw energy from my plight. She assured me my only problem was my attitude, and that I needed to prioritize "self-care." She got more and more impatient with me.

Finally, she said she was going to help me set some goals. "Get naked and look in the mirror," she said. "Really look. Can you honestly blame him for leaving? Now, make a list of the things you'd like to change and another list of the steps you're going to take to make that happen."

It seemed so empowering and responsible. "Maybe she's grown up," I thought, rummaging in a drawer for a permanent marker. Tracing it around bits of me I'd like to lop off, I imagined them melting away, and when I looked in the mirror, I imagined how I'd be without them. More like her.

She was a tough life coach. Whenever I complained about the lack of food, the gruelling exercise regimen, she would say, "Suck it up, buttercup. 'Faut souffrir pour être belle.' Beauty is pain."

She was so sophisticated, with her French phrases. When I looked in the mirror, I could almost see her, just behind me, egging me on to be my best self. Oh god, I got faint just thinking about eggs. But she got me presents, too, like an exercise bike, and a precise scale to measure my progress, and some fashion magazines to inspire me.

After a couple of months, she didn't seem so friendly. For one thing, she was in my head 24/7. When I looked in the mirror, she was always there, pointing out all the parts that were still too round. We spent a lot of time fighting. She got very upset when I told her I was too tired to exercise. But she promised that when I got down below ninety pounds, she'd get me something extra special.

It was so exciting when the scale read 88.7 one morning. And I felt great. Not hungry at all. Ketosis is like a miracle. I was a demon on the exercise bike. True, my breath smelled like nail polish remover, but hey, "Faut souffrir."

She was over the moon. Right away she sent me the special gift, just like she promised. It was a magnifying mirror. 20x magnification with optical glass for clear focus on one side, normal reflection on the other. I mounted it next to the bed, so we could start to totally make over my face to fit my new body.

When I woke up just before dawn the next morning, I felt disoriented, but just as determined as ever. I pulled the mirror over to start working on my face, and then I just got lost. In high quality 20x magnification, my dry, blotchy complexion was like a lunar landscape, my crow's feet like crevasses. I wandered around in the blue black pits under my eyes. I squeezed a pimple, and it erupted like a volcano.

Her voice startled me. "Hey! Thunder Thighs. Get up and on that bike. What are you thinking?"

This wasn't like before, when I knew what she would say in my head. The voice was right next to me, and as she spoke, she reached over my shoulder and swung the mirror hard into my forehead.

I was already feeling weak, and I must have blacked out. When I came to, I immediately looked in the mirror. There she was, looking back at me. She was thin, tan, and smiling, glamorous as a Hollywood movie star. I tried to reach out to touch the fur trim on the collar of her robe, but my fingers hit glass. I pushed my face towards hers, but again, there was glass between us.

She laughed at me.

I didn't understand. "What's wrong? I did everything you said."

She kept laughing, a long, silvery peal, and she threw her head back so I could appreciate her curls and the fine column of her neck. "Yes. I suppose I should thank you," she said at last. "I haven't felt so alive since—my last pageant, I guess. This little project of ours has completely revived me.

"But you—there's hardly anything left of you, poor dear. You better just rest. I've got a lot of living to do, and I can't be dragged down by a pathetic, worthless—"

She put her hand out and pushed me away. Only when I felt myself swinging back against the wall did I realize she had trapped me in the mirror. I panicked, feeling the mirror world close in on me. But I didn't ask her for help, and I wouldn't, never again. Somewhere deep inside, I still had some pride.

Her vanity was her undoing. She got all made up to go out, but she just had to check every detail of her makeup before she put on her glamorous gown. Flicking on the mirror light, she turned the magnifying side up towards her face. Maybe she didn't realize I'd still be there—and stronger by a factor of 20x.

I punched my fist through and gouged her eye. She reached for me, too. Remorselessly, our fingers dug around the gelatinous bulb, nails piercing the thin skin of the eyelid, fingertips plunging, grasping tough fibrous muscles, bathing in the rich, thick gore spurting everywhere. Screaming and writhing, we were locked together in the pain and the power of our struggle. We both knew it would go on and on and never stop until, at last, ripping the optic nerve, we drew the eyeball forth in triumph.

It was over, and she had retreated somewhere. After the throat tearing noise, the stillness rang in my ears. Holding her eyeball tenderly, I got out of bed and went over to the full length mirror. She was lurking in there, but she didn't look like a movie star anymore. Sludgy, dark blood flowed slowly from her empty eye socket. She was skin and bones. Her stringy hair was a mess, and she had lost her robe. She was wearing a workout tank and yoga pants that hung off her in bloody, baggy folds. I held up her eyeball, and she held up mine in a terrible pact. She could never look down on me again. We were equals.

"We can both be strong now," I told her. "Pain is beauty."

CELYN THE EXILE
SONS OF THE SPIDER-GOD
A SWORD AND SORCERY NOVELLA
LORENZO D. LOPEZ

WHEN ELEPHANTS FLY by Carlton Herzog

I

Only when the sweet summer trees grow full do the flying elephants descend to graze in Yakkaloosa county, and then only for a time. Zoologists remain baffled as to how they acquired wings, let alone how those wings can propel those majestic bulks aloft. Nor do they know from whence they come nor where they go after they leave. But as extraordinary as these flying pachyderms may seem, they are but one of many mysteries now common in this Age of Enigmas, where the seemingly impossible has become routine.

At the outset, opinions varied: the fanciful saw the hand of magic; the scientific saw aerodynamics and evolution abruptly upended; the catastrophist saw portents of doom; the cynic a hoax.

The elephants' arrival and departure always coincided with oddities in the planet Neptune's orbit and luminosity. During those times, astronomers studying the vibrant blue behemoth watched in awe as Neptune's dynamic planetwide storm system abated. They did not make the connection between aberrant elephants and the planet's curious behaviour.

One man would, though by chance and not scientific rigor. Pablo Ortiz, about whom this story revolves, worked as a financier at Goldman Sachs' New York office. He counted himself a numbers man, existentially defined and regulated by the very algorithms he used in his work. To his mind, sceptically empirical in the extreme, the idea of flying elephants had a fairy tale quality. As did other bizarre claims gaining currency, such as Sudden Onset Three Eye Syndrome, or SOTES as it came to be known. He attributed the whole thing to the law of vacant minds: empty heads abhor a vacuum and compulsively fill themselves with nonsense the way overeaters do junk food.

On Monday, June 10, 2058, Pablo had a change of heart. On Sunday, June 9, he had gone to bed with two good eyes, and woke the next day with three. As that enormous third eye stared back at him in the mirror, perched as it was above and between his two birth eyes, and pulsing with a life, and perhaps a sentience of its own, Pablo was forced to be more open minded about the improbable.

Nevertheless, he came to loathe that bulging carnival eye. For years, he had been regarded as an exceptionally handsome man, but now the only thing people saw when they looked at him was that cyclopean green orb jutting from his forehead.

Pablo's third eye didn't just taint his social standing; it discoloured and warped his mind. For example, while his two birth eyes would see the world as discrete objects, his third eye saw it as one big Mandelbrot set: a composite of fractured self similar geometries that repeated themselves at smaller and smaller scales; little bulbs piled on big bulbs festooned with double spirals, double hooks, islands, valleys and antennae.

At first, his employer, Goldman Sachs, proved sympathetic. The company went so far as to hide him in the company's file room, so he could not interact with the public. But his appearance so repulsed what few employees he encountered the company let him go with a modest severance package. After that, he could find no work. To avoid the stares and ridicule, he avoided public places and always travelled in disguise with a broad brimmed hat pulled low on his forehead.

He was not alone: Sudden Onset Third Eye Syndrome (SOTES) had become a minor epidemic. As the number of SOTES afflicted persons grew, so did society's hostility toward them. Hate groups targeted them for beatings while even the most liberal minded progressives stood on the side lines and did nothing to prevent the mob violence.

Pablo found himself crushed between his own self-loathing and society's. One night, as he wandered aimlessly about town, he spotted the Professor Fumbl's *Peace of Mind Bookstore*. The man behind the counter also had a third eye. Little remained of his birth eyes since they had receded into his face to the point of mere slits. As Pablo approached him, the man smiled and pointed to his own protuberant third eye:

The man asked, "You have questions?"

Pablo said, "This eye just showed up on my forehead. And my other two seem to be getting smaller. I look like a cyclops."

The man smiled again and said, "Did you know that Neptune's son Polyphemus had two empty eye sockets between which sat a great third eye? The Romans considered him to be a super being who protected the weak, represented metaphorically as sheep. They regard his great eye as a shield against evil."

Pablo scoffed. "Myth and fairy tales that have no place in the 21st century."

The man said, "There are many here that believe Neptune is a very real being, one that casts his influence over our world. Why do you suppose that Neptune has monuments in Poland, Berlin, Nuremburg, Florence, New York, Washington and Paris? Tomorrow is July 23, the Neptunalia. There will be festivals all over the world celebrating Neptune.

"I believe that you have been marked as a Son of Neptune. The Great Blue Orb has been known to mark its children with special gifts."

Pablo said angrily, "This optical cancer is simply an eruption of randomness on my forehead. Particles pop in and out of existence all the time. Consider that one minute there was nothing, no matter, no space, and the next voila, a universe full of stars and planets and you and me. And now our Third Eyes."

The man said, "Shit doesn't just happen. We live in a universe of cause and effect."

Pablo said, "Yes, shit does. If you could ask a turkey who has been well fed the day before Thanksgiving what the morrow will bring, he—fooled by the illusion of regularity—would answer 'More of the same of course.' Like the turkey, you assume that repetition is a boundary condition, that the past is predictive of the future. Nothing could be further from the truth."

"Consider that on rare occasions, evolution proceeds very rapidly to form new families, orders and classes of organisms. Stephen Jay Gould called that phenomenon 'punctuated equilibrium' and the creatures it produces hopeful monsters. If the first living thing that developed a working eye could talk, it would probably offer up a supernatural explanation as absurd as yours; the same holds true for the first fish that crawled on land, the first bird whose wings enabled it to fly, and the first primate to walk upright."

"So, it's a puzzle, not a divine act; it's wily, capricious Nature not some trident wielding fish loving deity of old."

The man said, "Those are human approximations of something beyond our comprehension. At this moment, Neptune manifests as the eighth planet in our solar system."

Pablo asked, "Are you kidding me? Look here, Professor Fumbles McStupid, Neptune is 2.8 billion miles away. It's the most distant object in the solar system. It's made of hydrogen, helium and methane wrapped around water, ammonia and ice. It's blue because the methane absorbs red light. Its winds whip around at 600 metres per second. How you go from that to an old guy with a beard, riding a dolphin, is the hallmark of delusional thinking."

The man smiled and said, "The planet is its disguise. Who can say what it really is? An exotic form of intelligent life, perhaps. It is not alone; it has brethren in other star systems as we are now discovering. We call them Neptune as well. Because we live on a placid island of ignorance floating in a sea of stars, we assume man—bipedal, opposable thumbs, mildly smarter than a chimpanzee—is the apex of creation. What if a Neptune sits higher on the food chain; what if its subharmonic murmurs through the void influence our development here? A life and will of its own, an inorganic consciousness, capable of genetic puppetry that even now guides and enforces our biological evolution."

Pablo asked, "Well that's a mouthful of bizarro xenobiology if I ever heard some. Let's dial down the crazy and give me some practical advice on how to navigate this world while looking like I just jumped out of Homer's *Odyssey*."

The man said, "Since you raised the question, let me answer it with a quote from Odysseus himself:

Let no man ever live contrary to what is customary and right,

But accept in silence the gifts of the gods whatever they may bring.

II

Pablo left the Peace of Mind bookstore more agitated than when he entered. He hadn't gone more than a few blocks when he was surrounded by a group of ruffians. At first, they were content to mock him as a freak. Then came the shoving and the spitting, followed by the kicks and punches.

He was not a violent person, nor given to fits of rage. But this attack was the straw that broke the camel's back. As he ducked away from the blows, he could feel his third eye pulsing and burning. His whole body felt electric. He turned and faced his assailants. As he did, his eye projected an intense beam of otherworldly light. That light fractalized and incinerated his assailants.

Pablo stood there amazed. The third eye he despised had just saved him from a terrific beating. It wasn't just a window into the hidden nature of things. It was also a weapon capable of incredible power.

He returned home. He stared at the walls, his mind empty of thought or affect. He heard a knock. When he opened the door, he found two men in black suits. They introduced themselves as Mr. Smith and Mr. Jones. They said they needed his help. Pablo got scared. He assumed they knew about the recent disintegration of the hooligans. He breathed a deep sigh of relief when they didn't raise the issue.

Mr. Smith said, "We're with Longevity Pharmaceuticals. About a year ago, an Air Force F 35 mistook the elephants for a Russian spy plane and shot one down. Under contract, we did the autopsy. We found a heretofore unknown hormone, longevinine. It slows human aging down to a crawl. We haven't been able to replicate it in the laboratory. Our employer believes that given enough time and test subjects we will be able to manufacture it by the boatload and corner the market."

"That's where your third eye enters the picture. At the molecular level, the elephants exhibit fractal combinations. We believe that those same patterns would present in their exhalations as a gaseous trail of fractals. Our instruments aren't sufficiently sensitive to acquire that trail. But your eye, we believe could. Mind you, we have employed others with SOTES to find the elephants. But we've had no success. Either because the candidates lacked the ability to do it or didn't want to betray a group of fellow mutants."

Mr. Jones, said, "Can you help us? We'll make it worth your while."

Depressed and unemployed, Pablo felt the offer seemed like the perfect balm for his economic and emotional wounds.

"Of course I will," he said.

After that the elephant hunt began in earnest. It began in Yakkaloosa County. Pablo and a team of Longevity's scientists and security people flew by helicopter along a trail only Pablo could see. During the expedition, one of the guards bragged to the other about hunting African elephants.

The guard seated next to Pablo said, "I made a killing over there. Ivory prices have gone through the roof because it's so rare. The governments over there try their best, but hunters like me know the ropes and can get at them with bribes."

The guard across from Pablo said, "Yeah. That will probably happen with the flying ones. Sooner than later since Congress is dragging its feet about protective legislation."

Pablo listened and said nothing. He thought to himself: *If the elephants contain some rare chemical in their bodies, it stands to reason that three eyed people might as well. That means these pricks could be hunting my kind next. What have I got myself into here?*

By now, the chopper was over the remote Lake of Woods in Minnesota. That's when they saw the portal, a large shimmering circle of light dancing above the calm water. Pablo said, "The vapor trail leads into that doorway. If you want to find them, then fly into it."

There was a moment's hesitation, then the pilot pushed the joystick forward and the chopper flew inside. The lake was gone. And so was the earth. They were approaching what was obviously the planet Neptune. A moment later, they were flying over the planet's methane blue skies. At the time, the chopper pilot and all his astronomically ignorant passengers, save one, had no idea where they were. The newly christened Son of Neptune did. He informed the crew.

Although they were skimming across the skies of the eighth planet in the solar system, they felt no chill, no lack of oxygen, no excess of gravity. It was a terrestrial corridor cut through Neptune's hydrogen, helium and methane atmosphere.

The pilot spotted a small earth like landmass ahead, along with an enormous herd of flying elephants grazing there. Everyone in the chopper offered explanations as to the how and why of their journey to the eighth planet, their ability to survive the brutal conditions there, and how the elephants had been given or had carved out an oasis in that frigid blue hell.

Smith was the first of offer an insight: "There's more to the elephants than meets the eye. It's not just the wings and gravity defying abilities. It's mental teleportation and mental terraforming as well. This goes way beyond extending life."

Jones took it one step further: "If the elephants have hidden talents, I'll bet our friend Pablo does as well."

Pablo demurred, not wanting to disclose his disintegrator eye beams. He felt it wise to play the part of a loyal team member until he could decide on a course of action.

He said, "Not that I'm aware of. I suspect more will be revealed. But shouldn't we head back now that we know where they roost. We can come back with the means to capture or kill as many as we want."

They took Pablo's suggestion and flew back through the portal. When they touched down, the Longevity team began formulating a plan of action. For his part, Pablo inched away from the chopper as the animated dialogue reached a fever pitch.

When he felt that he was far enough away, he focused his third eye on the group and the helicopter directly behind them. He concentrated. Hard. Until he felt his body seethe with that eldritch force he had felt before.

This time there was no time gap between the fractalization and disintegration process. A blinding blue light exploded from Pablo's eye. It vaporized the tarmac between him and the helicopter, and everything thereafter for a mile in three of the remaining compass directions.

Investigators categorized it as an asteroid impact as powerful as the one that struck Tunguska, Russia, in 1908.

Pablo didn't waste any time. He called an Uber. He meant to obliterate Longevity Pharmaceuticals, for he knew that the helicopter team had reported its finding to corporate. He wanted to ensure that no one knew of the elephant's secret habitat on Neptune.

In later years, Pablo moved himself into the woods around the elephant's Yakkaloosa feeding ground. He lived off the land. He spoke to no one.

He waited as the elephant's self-appointed protector. Every now and then he would obliterate snooping reporters or scientists, as well as any civilian or military aircraft presenting the slightest possibility of harm to his wards. He was their steward secure in the knowledge that whatever caused him to grow that third eye, be it design or accident, did not do so in vain.

The proprietor of the Peace of Mind Bookstore was right. More was revealed. He was a hopeful monster pointing toward a new evolutionary path, one less hostile to the other creatures of the earth. He was a true Son of Neptune.

GAVIN CHAPPELL

Sinbad

AND THE

VIKING QUEEN

BLOODY PALM by Justin Fleischman

Derek jogs completely up the steep road. Once at the top of Berry Road, he places his hands on his knees, taking several deep breaths. This is the fifth time he's run up this road. He plans on doing it two more times.

He turns then walks down the hilly road at a fast pace, glancing at the white house with a wooden porch.

"I can make this two more times," he quietly says, rubbing sweat from his eyes. He jogged up the lengthy road six times two days ago. He's trying to increase his sprints by one each time he runs.

He started running again due to the closure of the Brick Wall Gym, where he lifted weights four days a week, due to Covid 19.

With the gym's doors being temporarily shut, he needs to do something to keep in shape.

Once reaching the bottom of the hill, he turns and starts jogging. Then his cell rings. He stops, taking it from his pocket.

Holly

He immediately answers his ex-wife's call. "Yeah, what is it?"

"Derek, would it be okay if I picked up Aiden a little earlier than usual Sunday evening?"

"Are you freaking kidding me, Holly?" His eyes open wide as he shouts. Aiden is their ten year old son who stays with Derek during the weekends. "What's so important that I have to spend less time with my son?"

"Hailey's coming in this weekend. She wants to spend time with her nephew."

"Your sister wants to visit with her nephew, she can drop by my place." He shakes his head. "Don't have a problem with her stopping over."

"Derek," she sighs, "we shouldn't make house visits with the coronavirus going around."

Then why's your sister coming to visit from two states over? Derek gargles then spits. He runs his left hand threw his longer than usual curly brown hair before replying. "As usual, Holly, you're right. Tell me what time to bring him back Sunday and I'll cut my time with him short to do it."

"Der, it'll only be two or three hours before you usually drop him off."

He gazes up the road, feeling in no mood to finish his workout—or continue this conversation. "Whatever you want, dear." He disconnects then walks up the hill. One of the many things he'd learned to do since his divorce is know when to quit speaking.

Approaching the small, yellow rental house he lives in, he removes his phone and presses the Facebook App. He notices a Friend Request from a woman named Rory Rouchburt. Her lips are ruby red. She has bright blue eyes and long, straight brown hair. "Pretty cute." He doesn't know her, but presses Add Friend.

"Rory Rouchburt." Unlocking the front door, he laughs. "Sounds like a stripper's name."

Derek receives a message: *Rory Rouchburt Accepted Your Friend Request.* That's odd. Thought she requested me for a friend.

He looks at the original message. It doesn't say *Sent You A Friend Request* it reads: *Suggested Friend Request.* Derek laughs, wondering who their mutual friends are. He flips down Facebook and notices two different pictures of Rory. In one, she has her hair tied to the sides, her ruby red lips still noticeable. The other is a side view. Her hair is down with the question added: *Does my hair look flat?*

Derek responds: *Your hair looks good—don't worry about it.*

He grabs a Diet Coke from the refrigerator then is watching a movie on television when a reply comes from

Rory. *Derek Cronshaw you're so sweet* ☐. *But I need to do something with my hair!*

He types: *You look beautiful!*

Not receiving a reply after ten minutes, he stands, goes into the kitchen and removes another bottle of Diet Coke from the refrigerator.

After taking a large gulp of his drink, his phone dings. He notices it's a message from Rory.

I haven't been working. Damn coronavirus!

He smiles. *That sucks. I'll buy you dinner sometime. Help out anyway I can.*

After sending the message, he believes it quite forward. He sets the phone on the arm rest.

Her response comes through minutes later.

I live with my aunt.

What's that got to do with anything? he thinks. Well, maybe she just wants to change the subject.

He starts into another message. *Okay, I can take you and your aunt out.*

The screen shows bubbles.

You really want to take my aunt out? LOL!

He laughs. *Not really. Just want to meet you.*

She replies: *Nothing's open.*

He sips his drink, changing channels with the remote.

The whistle blows inside the garage. Derek, operating a forklift, lowers a large package into the back of the truck. He backs up the forklift, parks it, removes a hankie from his pocket then wipes his face.

Entering the break room, he pours a cup of coffee. Sipping it, he removes his phone.

Opening Facebook, he sees a picture of Rory in pigtails, wearing a pink bikini top. His eyes open wide while his tongue slides across his teeth.

Pretty

Her comment appears minutes later:

Thank you! ♥ So sweet!

He switches to instant messenger, goes to her name and types:

Okay if I have your number so I can call you sometime?

Almost two hours later, Rory replied: *Sorry, I fell asleep. Just Instant Message for now.*

Derek arranges the boxes in the truck.

Derek steps out of his Nissan, carrying two plastic bags. One holds two Cherry Coke Zero two litres the others contains a half–pound of roast beef lunch meat, a bottle of bar-b-que sauce and a half dozen eggs.

Once in the house, he sets the groceries on the table. Putting them into the refrigerator, he sighs. I really need to stop eating and drinking this garbage.

Still, he takes a glass from the cabinet to pour the drink into. Then he sits in his chair, sips from the glass, removes his iPhone and goes to Instant Messenger.

If you and your aunt would feel safe coming to my place one evening, I'll make dinner. That would really make me happy. Promise to stay six feet away from you both. I haven't had much company since my divorce.

After hitting send, he sits the phone on the armrest, stands, unplugs his iPad that rested on the coffee table and skims through the local news.

Then Rory responds:

Okay, sounds fun! We ain't been getting out much neither. Really getting cabin fever! LOL! What are you making to eat?

Hadn't thought about that. Whatever you'd like, Rory.

Finishing his soda, he goes into the kitchen and fills his glass.

Derek has never been much of a cook. He remembers grilling steaks and chicken on the grill at his old house—his ex-wife's current house. But since living alone, he'd usually fry burgers, cook spaghetti and eat canned vegetables.

Turning on the television, he searches for an On Demand movie to watch. Then a message comes through from Rory.

We like Italian food! Do you like Italian food? We would love an Italian dinner!

He grins, thinking she might be as excited as he is.

Since Holly wants to have Aiden back early Sunday, he believes that day would work.

I can make Italian food. I have my son this weekend, but he'll be going back to his mother's Sunday afternoon. Would Sunday evening, about six be good?

He waits for her response. The bubbles show then disappear. After nearly five minutes, her reply shows.

Let me ask my aunt.

Why does she have to check with her aunt? What's this lady's story? He sighs, shaking his head. This is freaking weird. Shit, maybe she's still a teenager. I never checked her age.

While he watches the action movie *The Night Clerk*, he gets a message.

Aunt Pearl said Sunday is good for us. You said you're making Italian Food? That sounds great!

He laughs, then replies: *Anytime between 5 and 6 is good*—then he gives his address.

Unsure if Rory will send anything back, he immediately calls Holly. It rings twice before going to voicemail.

"Holly, sorry I snapped during our conversation. I do think it important Aiden spends time with his aunt. Whatever time you want me to drop him off at the house Sunday, I'll do it."

After disconnecting, he resumes watching the movie. It's been a while since he had something, besides spending time with his son, to look forward to.

At 2:00pm Sunday, Derek pulls into the driveway of his former house. Aiden, sitting in the passenger seat, unlatches his seatbelt. This is the first time Derek let Aiden sit upfront. He believes his son's old enough.

"Thanks for bringing me home, Daddy."

Derek bites his lip, thinking about when it'd been both of their homes. "You're welcome, buddy. I really enjoy spending time with you on the weekends."

Aiden hugs his father. Derek kisses his cheek. "Have fun with your Aunt Hailey."

Aiden smiles at his father before departing the car. They wave to each other as Derek backs out of the driveway.

On the drive home, he pulls into the small DeSalvo's' Supperette. Parking, he takes out his phone, gets on the Internet and looks up the menu for the restaurant *Italian Cooking.*

He knew all along it'd be smarter to support this restaurant during these tough times than to try and prepare and authentic Italian dinner himself.

He then calls the restaurant and orders two pounds of spaghetti and meatballs, Zucchini planks, cheesy garlic bread, veal and salad then enters the store to purchase a 2liter of Diet Coke.

At 6:20, Derek gazes out his bedroom window. A small, blue car creeps along the road then pulls into the driveway. He rushes into the kitchen where the spaghetti and meatballs are kept warm in the oven and the zucchini planks and veal are heated on the burner with the salad in a large bowl on the counter. The doorbell rings. He moves to the door.

He expects to see Rory upon opening the door, but her aunt stands there.

"Hello, Derek Cronshaw?" the aunt asks. Rory, wearing blue rimmed glasses, stands behind her.

"Yes." He smiles.

"I'm Rory's Aunt Pearl." She shakes his hand. Her hand is bigger than his. "Pearl Davison."

"Come in." They release hands. He moves out of the way so Pearl will enter. He then sees Rory and stares at her pink jeans. Then she faces him, smiling. "You have a nice house."

Derek grins. "Thanks. Hope you like the food. I picked it up from a restaurant, *Italian Cooking*."

Keeping her smile, she says nothing and goes inside the house.

"So, you live here by yourself?" Rory turns and asks him.

"Yeah," he closes the door, "most of the time. My son's here on weekends."

"Did you prepare all this food yourself?" Pearl asks from the kitchen.

"No," Derek laughs—wanting to build whatever it is he's getting into on honesty. "I was at the creek with my son most of the day—didn't have time to cook. I bought it from the restaurant, *Italian Cooking*."

"It's really nice meeting you." Rory sticks out her hand. As Derek shakes it, he realises it's even frailer than he expected. Unlike her aunt, Rory is thin.

"So, would you like to watch a movie later on?" Derek asks. "I don't have Netflix. I watch movies On Demand."

Rory glances to the side, blinking. "Could you show me how to pick an On Demand movie?"

Thought everybody knew how to do that. "Yes, Rory, no problem."

"Hope you don't mind us coming into your house without wearing a mask." Rory sits on the couch. "I hate them. Can't breathe wearing those fucking things."

Derek chuckles at her expletive then sits directly beside her. "They're a real hassle sometimes." He shows her the free On Demand movies then hands her the remote control.

"Derek, may I speak to you for a minute?" Pearl asks from behind the couch while Rory skims through the movies.

Derek stands then moves behind the couch to see Pearl.

"In private," she quietly says. Her and Derek go into the kitchen then sit in the two chairs at the table. Derek realizes he didn't add another chair. "Okay, I know it's very strange for your date to come here with her aunt."

"No problem." He shakes his head.

"You see, Derek," Pearl cranks her neck to look out of the kitchen's entranceway. "Rory was in a car accident, a little over two years ago with her mom and dad. Her mother and father died in it."

His jaw drops.

"Rory suffered a severe brain injury. She knows what happened—but doesn't remember it happening—if that makes sense."

Derek stares into her eyes. "I'm very sorry."

"I moved into my late sister and brother in law's house shortly after that. Rory'd been in therapy for six months. I'd been taking care of her since then."

"That's very commendable of you." His head drops.

"It's my life now." She sits back, her dark, curly hair covering the side of her face. "Her old friends, well, they don't look at or treat her quite the same anymore. And, well, I get a little paranoid when she makes new friends."

He wonders if it'd be appropriate to ask questions.

"She's twenty four, but sometimes, she'll act like a girl much younger." She sighs. "She doesn't behave the way she used to."

Derek gazes down and to his side. "I have a ten year old son. Don't know what I'd do if something like that ever happened to him."

Derek and Pearl then go into the living room. Rory is skimming through the movies.

"Did you find a movie you like, honey?" Pearl sits beside her.

"Don't think so." She slightly shakes her head, eyes fixed on the television screen.

"Well, don't worry about that right now." Pearl takes the remote from her hand. "We're going to eat now."

"We'll find something to watch after we eat." Derek smiles.

Rory stands and goes into the kitchen. Derek and Pearl follow her.

Derek enters the pantry, removes a folding chair and places it at the table then takes three plates from the cabinet.

After eating, they watch a free On Demand movie, *Dumb and Dumber*. Derek relaxes in his chair. Rory and Pearl sit on the couch.

Derek glances at Rory each time she laughs at the picture's corny jokes. Knowing what she'd went through doesn't change his feelings. He still wants to see her again—preferably without the aunt. But knows, especially with the quarantine, it's unlikely.

Pearl asks Derek about his job. He tells her about his duties of packing the trailers for semi-trucks. He peeks at Rory, who smiles, watching the movie and wonders if she is even capable of holding a job.

Rory removes her Droid from her back pocket. She glances at Derek then looks at her phone. "What's your number, Derek?"

As he gives it to her, he watches Pearl from the corner of his eye. She gazes down, slightly smiling.

"What's yours, Rory?" he asks.

His phone rings.

"You have it." She holds up her phone, a large smile on her face. "But don't bug me too much." She laughs.

"Try not to." He saves the number.

After the movie, Pearl slings her purse over her shoulder. "Thanks for inviting us over, Derek. You're a nice gentleman."

Derek smirks. "Thank you."

Rory's arms spread and her eyes open wide. "Do we have to leave, Aunt Pearl? Why can't we watch another movie? I'm having fun."

"Honey, Derek has to work in the morning," Pearl says. "And you probably can't stay awake for another one. You two have each other's numbers now, you'll speak again soon."

Derek nods. *Yeah, hopefully without you around.*

"I had a job." Rory turns to Derek. "I rang the Salvation Army bell outside Target."

Pearl goes toward the door. "Thanks again, Derek. Appreciate you spending time with Rory."

"She's a very nice young lady." He tries thinking of a compliment for Pearl—knowing he can't call her a young lady. "Uh, great meeting you both."

"Oh," Rory smiles at him, "what I'd said before, about 'bugging me too much,' I was joking."

Derek grins. Pearl walks out the door. Rory follows.

Derek moves to the window and watches them enter the car and drive away. Then he grabs his phone and gets on Facebook to see what 'mutual friends' he and Rory have.

The first is Rob Canner, a guy he used to work with and hasn't seen in a while. The other is his ex-wife's cousin Jason. He knows not to bother either one of them over this.

As Derek drives home from work, a text comes through. He glances at his charging phone lying on the passenger seat.

Rory

He drives home before reading the text.

Hey, buddy! Sorry we left early yesterday. But I had fun!

He laughs. *You didn't leave early. We had dinner and watched a funny movie. I had a good time too.*

He sees the bubbles and knows she must be replying.

Derek's in his bedroom, tossing his dirty pants onto the floor when his phone dings. He looks at Rory's text.

We should meet up again. But nothing's open.

After reading it, he sets the phone on the dresser then strolls into the bathroom. His cell beeps again so he goes back to the bedroom.

Ever been to Butterfly Falls? It's off the highway. Used to go there a lot before.

Is she asking me out on a date at Butterfly Falls? Sure hope Auntie doesn't come. He types: *I know just what you're referring to. Drove past it, never been back there before.*

He sets the phone down then goes into the shower before another text can stop him.

Minutes after showering, Rory's latest text shows.

Let's go there! Ain't been there in I don't know how years.

Derek knows she meant to type 'how many years.' *Okay. How's Saturday? I can bring my son if we go then.*

He wonders how his son will take to Rory and Pearl—and vice versa.

Aiden gets into the back of the Nissan wearing blue and yellow Pokémon swim trunks and fastens his seatbelt.

Derek enters the driver's side then smiles at his son in the rear view mirror. "Don't want to sit up front like a big boy?"

"Mommy says I sit in the back."

"Yeah." He looks forward then inserts the key into the ignition. "She's right." He thinks about when he picked Aiden up the day before and Aiden sat in the back of the car. He didn't say anything then. He wishes he hadn't said anything now.

"Where we going swimming, Daddy?" Aiden stares outside the window.

"Place called Butterfly Falls," he reminds him. "I didn't tell you, Aiden, we're meeting two of Daddy's new friends there."

"Boys or girls?" Aiden asks.

Derek's eyes widen upon hearing that. "They're ladies. Why do you ask?"

"Sometimes, Mommy's new friends are boys when I thought they'd be girls."

Derek says nothing.

Derek pulls off the four lane road, into the gravel parking lot. Only a red truck is there.

Once he shuts off the vehicle, Aiden unbuckles his seatbelt then opens the door. Derek steps out, wearing his grey and white trunks and a collarless and sleeveless blue shirt. He wipes perspiration from his forehead, looking at Aiden, who stares at the big wooden sign reading: *Butterfly Falls Natural Park* in blue letters with three different coloured butterflies painted on it.

Aiden turns. "We going into the woods, Daddy? That where the lake is?"

Derek nods, glancing at the road. "In a minute, bud." He sucks in his gut as the blue car pulls in.

Rory and her aunt speak for over a minute until Rory leaves the car, wearing a pink bikini and sunglasses.

"Hello, Derek." Her arms spread, holding a pink towel in one hand, cell phone in the other.

Pearl backs up then drives away.

"Rory." He smiles—surprised and happy Pearl isn't staying. He looks at his son, who walks toward him. "Aiden, this is my friend, Rory Rouchburt. Rory, my son, Aiden."

Rory crouches to eyelevel with Aiden then removes her sunglasses. "Nice meeting you, Aiden. You ready to swim in the lake?"

"Good meeting you too, Rory." He extends his hand, smiling. She shakes it. "Have you been here before? Is it fun?"

Derek smiles, feeling Aiden has good manners.

"I think it's fun, Aiden. Hope you do too." She stands.

Another car pulls into the lot. Aiden leads the way as they walk between the trees and along the path. Derek and Rory stay a few feet behind him, hearing the babbling brook beyond the trees to the left.

"Used to warn us about snakes here." Rory looks at the trees. "Snakes don't really scare me, though."

"They don't?" Derek watches his son.

"No. Don't know if I've ever even seen a snake. I hate crabs though. Those ugly things scare the shit out of me."

"Yeah?" Derek laughs.

"Yeah. Had a bad experience with them when I was a little girl. I was at a beach with mom and dad. I stupidly wandered away from them. Came upon, I don't know, five or six crabs on the beach and freaked out. Felt like those ugly things were staring at me. I ran back crying. When I saw my parents they were—I mean I could tell by their faces, they were scared. I thought it was because I saw crabs. But they said it was because they didn't know where I was."

They come to an upward slant. Railroad ties are fastened into the earth, making a stairway. Aiden stretches his legs onto the wood going up the trail.

"You okay walking, buddy?" Derek asks his son, hearing him grunt.

"Yes," Aiden answers.

"I came here when I was in high school." Rory puts her sunglasses on. "Changed since then. Used to be here a lot with my friends. But I don't see old friends much anymore."

Derek nods, remembering her aunt telling him about how her old friends react different to her since the accident.

They turn a corner and walk further up the trail. Rory rubs her hand along the wooden fence on the left that comes up to her shoulders. They then see water falling twenty to twenty five feet from a cliff into a large pool.

"This is really nice!" Derek says. "Had no idea it's like this back here."

"Can I go into the water, Dad?" Aiden removes his shirt.

"Yeah, go ahead." Derek answers, staring at two guys swimming near the waterfall. Then he hears a man and a woman laughing, walking along the path.

"Come on, Der, let's get in the water." Rory kicks off her flip flops, takes off her sunglasses, drops them then slowly walks into the water with Aiden. "Burr, this is cold."

Derek chuckles, watching his son bend his knees then splash water onto his head. "Chill doesn't seem to bother Aiden." He removes his sandals and shirt then goes into the water. Stepping on several small stones, he gets waist length into the water. "A little cold, but we'll get used to it."

Rory floats on her back, then backstrokes further out. She stands, then moves closer to Derek and hugs him. "It's colder in the deep end."

He wraps her in his arms and they move deeper into the water. Rory encloses her legs around his waist—Derek smiles, still watching his son. Aiden dunks his head in and out of the water—laughing.

He faces Rory. She stares into his eyes. "I haven't been with a woman since my divorce."

She opens her mouth, slightly. Derek kisses her.

Keeping her in his arms, he looks at the top of the waterfall. A young man stands at the top of it, spreading out his arms then he jumps from the top and lands inside the pool. After going under, he comes up laughing.

"Did you see that, Rory?" He faces her, smirking. "Kid jumped off the cliff into the water."

She kisses his lips.

After cooling off a little longer, Derek and Rory sit at the shore, keeping their feet in the water. Aiden does cannon balls off a ledge into the lake.

"Derek, since you invited us to your house, you can come to mine." Rory's head's down as she kicks her feet in the water.

"That'd be great." Derek watches his son.

"It's my house. That's what Mom and Dad say. But Aunt Pearl acts like it's her house. Pisses me off. Sometimes, I feel like I really don't need her around."

"You being careful, Aiden?" he asks as his son walks out of the water.

"Yes, Daddy." Aiden goes to the flat rock.

"Like, I needed to ask her if it's okay if I invited you over." She looks at him, eyes narrowed. "That's bullshit."

"She just wants what's best for you, Rory."

"But Mom and Dad say it's my house now."

Derek glances at her, eyes slanted then back at his son. *Aren't they deceased? Do you mean they* said *it's your house?*

Derek and Rory kiss near the Butterfly Falls Nature Area sign.

"I could drive you home." Derek kisses her neck.

"No," Rory laughs. "Aunt Pearl is on her way. Already texted her. But you'll come over for dinner."

"Yeah, I will." Derek meets her eyes, hearing Aiden laugh.

Minutes later, Pearl pulls in.

Rory rubs her hand on top of Aiden's head. "It was nice meeting you, handsome little guy. Your dad better bring you along again."

Derek smiles as Rory walks to the car, waving to him. Despite the Covid 19 affecting everything, he feels things are going well for him. He hadn't thought that in a while.

As the week goes on, Derek and Rory talk over the phone and text often. It consumes so much of Derek's life that he doesn't realize the news reporting the coronavirus cases are getting worse.

Friday evening he drives to Rory's house for a steak and potato dinner that Rory prepared.

After pulling into the single car driveway, he tosses two breath mints into his mouth. Shutting off the car, he walks to the cement sidewalk then to the blue house's door. After knocking once, Pearl opens the door.

"Hello, Derek. Glad you made it." She smiles then laughs. "Believe it or not, I have a date tonight too—if you want to call it that. Guy invited me to his house. Guess he's tired of being quarantined alone."

"Remember to stay six feet away. Oh," Derek pivots to view his car. "I'm sorry, I blocked you in. I'll move it." He goes back to his car then backs up. Pearl enters her car then leaves.

Derek didn't know Pearl intended to leave—and it makes him happy.

Opening the front door and stepping into the house, Rory is standing in the living room, wearing a blue bikini—different than the one she wore at Butterfly Falls. He smiles, staring at her medium sized breasts on her frail body.

"What do you think?" she asks. "This look better than the one I swam in? It feels better."

Derek cocks his head, still grinning.

"Bought this today while out with my aunt. Other one is getting too big on me. She said we may not be able to get out for a while."

This must be my lucky Friday night.

"Well," Rory spreads her arms, smiling, "do I look good in it?"

"Rory," he nods then moves toward her, "you look absolutely stunning in anything you wear."

Rory giggles as he kisses her neck, then moves to her lips. She leads him through the hall, into the bedroom. Derek unlatches his belt then unbuckles his pants.

Rory removes her bikini top as they fall onto the double bed.

"Hope my parents don't bother us." Rory removes Derek's shirt.

Derek kisses her—not thinking nor carrying about what she'd said.

Rory is still sleeping when Derek wakes. He runs his fingers across her smooth arm then kisses it.

He rises from the bed, puts on his pair of red and black boxers then walks to the kitchen.

Opening the refrigerator door, he's not surprised that what he wants, diet soda is not there. "This is better anyway." He removes a blue pitcher of water, opens the cupboards, searching for a glass. He finds one inside the third door he opens.

After pouring water into the glass, he takes a sip then notices something colourful moving outside the kitchen entranceway, then disappearing.

Didn't hear her get up. He walks through the kitchen. "Rory?"

He turns the corner. She's not there. "What the hell?"

He ventures into the living room, takes the remote controller and turns on the TV.

A Code Red Alert flashes on the screen for the viewing area, ordering residents to stay inside. "Son of a bitch." He finishes the water then walks into the kitchen to get more.

After filling his glass, he opens the refrigerator door. Then everything rumbles. He drops the jug of water. Much of it spills onto the white, porcelain floor and the shaking stops. He sprints from the kitchen.

"Rory! Rory!"

He enters the bedroom. She is still in bed asleep. As he moves toward her, there's a chill, then a whisper in his ear.

"Lustful heart."

He does a one eighty. No one is there. He pants and starts sweating.

"Derek, honey." Rory sits up in bed.

"The house shook!" His arms are in the air, eyes wide open. "You didn't feel that?"

She tilts her head, glaring at him.

He turns away. A yellow orb zips through the hall.

"Did you see that?" He turns to Rory—perspiration flows down his forehead and into his eyes. He wipes it away. "The house shook!"

Not waiting for her answer, he rushes into the hall and flicks on the light switch. A shadowy figure dashes by him and there's another cold chill. Still, sweat runs down his face.

"Rory, my God, there's something in your house!" He runs into the kitchen, picks up the water jug then drinks what little bit of water is left. Then the rumbling begins again—lasting a few seconds. "Damn it, what's going on? Need to get out!"

The yellow sphere appears before him. His teeth chatter. A vision of a bald man appears. His face has several wrinkles and his eyes are black. "Lustful heart," he says—but his slit of a mouth doesn't move.

"Leave me alone!" he screams.

The figure disappears. Rory enters the kitchen, wearing a blue nightgown. "What's wrong, Derek?"

"The house shook! Like there's a freaking earthquake. You had to feel it?"

She shakes her head. He realizes it'd only been the kitchen that shook.

"I saw a man! A bald man. He doesn't like me being here!"

Rory smiles with big eyes. "Daddy? You saw my daddy! I told Aunt Pearl, him and Mom, they're still here."

He sprints to the door and goes outside, leaving the door open.

As he makes it to his car, someone yells: "You go back inside!"

He slowly turns to his left. A man wearing a green and light brown shirt and hat approaches him.

"You've been ordered to stay inside," the national guardsman says. "Go back into the house you just came out of and put some damn clothes on!"

"Why?" Derek shivers. "I need to get out of here."

"Why?" The soldier places his hand on his pistol attached to his belt. "The coronavirus is at Level Red. Everyone is ordered to stay inside. Go back in!"

Derek quivers then slowly walks through the dusk back to the house. Panting as he tramples barefooted along the grass, he figures Pearl left because she knew something about this. Rory said she spoke about her father still being in the house and Pearl had not believed her. Or did she?

Stepping inside the house, he leaves the door open. Rory stares at him, head tilted.

"Where'd your aunt go?" He goes toward her then wraps his hands around her arms, shaking her. "Does she know what's here? Do you? Yes you do!"

"Derek—" She's quickly thrust back six feet. Then Derek is pushed to the floor. He lands hard, face first. His face is pushed onto the floor, breaking his nose and there's rumbling. He screams.

When the booming ceases, Derek gets to his knees. He wipes much blood from his face and busted nose. Then he feels blood in the hair on the back of his head and neck. He looks behind him. A bloody palm moves further away before disappearing.

Rory, sitting on the floor, stares at him, sobbing.

"What'd I do wrong? Why don't they..."

Suddenly, the room grows much colder. An older lady stands behind Rory. Blood gushes from the top of her head. Derek knows this is her mother.

He turns and goes out the door.

Once outside, Rory is out too. She clenches his arm with both her hands. "Please stay with me, Derek. They don't understand!"

He yanks his arm away then bolts into the yard.

The guard, standing in the middle of the road notices him. "Hey, I ordered you to stay inside! And you could be arrested right now for coming out in your underwear!"

Derek's head bows. He'd forgotten he only wore his boxers.

"I ordered you to get inside!" The national guardsman moves toward him. Derek turns and sprints to the house, wondering if there's a window on the house's other side he can crawl through.

Once he's inside, Rory screams.

"Damn it, Rory what's going on?"

She hollers again. Panting, Derek goes into the kitchen.

Five large crabs crawl on the wet floor. Rory stands against the wall, frozen.

"What the hell—"

"You brought those ugly things into the house! How could you? I told you they scare me, I hate them!"

"I didn't do it, Rory. Your parents put them there. They're—"

"Get them out!" she cries.

"They're not..." he wipes blood from his face and neck, "Shit, don't you see? Your parents want me out!"

"No!" She latches onto his arm so tightly that her fingernails pierce his flesh. Derek then sees Rory's mother and father, eyes and mouth bleeding, wearing torn clothing, standing in the puddle the crabs are walking in.

He hollers, shoving Rory to the floor. He races to her bedroom, shatters the window above her bed then leaps out and dashes through the yard.

"Don't leave me alone!" Rory screams. Derek knows she crawled out the window too.

He trips over bricks in the neighbours' yard then hits his right knee hard on the earth. Cursing, he wonders if Rory's parents had anything to do with the bricks being there.

"Derek, please come back!" Rory is still chasing him. "I'm so scared!"

He hears her panting and knows she is closer. He sprints to the next yard.

Sirens blare. He pays no attention to the noise and moves onto the road.

Getting almost halfway across the street, he sees headlights coming his way at a fast pace. A police car, with strobe lights flashing and blaring, pursues it, so he runs faster.

"Derek!"

He turns after crossing. Rory runs onto the road then falls down.

"Rory, no!" His eyes bulge and his hands are in the air.

As she tries standing, the speeding car blasts into her, sending her body flying several feet. She lands on the side of the road.

"No! Rory!" His sweaty hands cover his face. "Dear God, please don't let this be happening!"

The police car pulls over.

Derek collapses to his knees, believing there's no way Rory could've survived that hit, especially with the internal injuries she'd already suffered.

As the police officer goes to the body, Derek falls on his face, hopping the bloody palm will return and smash his skull into the ground.

Derek returns home after several hours at the police station. He'd told the police someone broke into the house and assaulted them both—because he knew they wouldn't believe the truth. Still, he knows this predicament is far from over.

As he lies in his bed, with a bandaged nose, the room is dark and tears run down his cheeks while he thinks about Rory. He only blames himself for her death. But now, perhaps she's with her mother and father in that house, heaven or hell or wherever they are.

He shuts his eyes. He opens them after he feels the coldest chill. Rory is standing at the edge of the bed. Her forehead is cut open and the wound grows larger going to her skull. One of her eyes is puffed up and sealed shut. Blood flows from her lips.

Derek wants to run out of the room and flee the house. But he knows it will do no good. Rory will haunt him no matter where he is for as long as she deems fit.

WITCH-QUEEN OF THE LOST RACE

by Rex Mundy

TUG by Douglas Ogurek

"Let's have a feast and celebrate. For this son of mine was
dead and is alive again; he was lost and is found."
     – Luke 15:24

I was taking a shit when Pullins walked in. He just stood
on the other side of my stall door, and did that damn
peekaboo whistle. I'd just started, and he did it the
whole time.

When I came out, he tore off a piece of duct tape.
"Poom. For a little guy, you got some mean, mean shit."
He was taping a "Friends and Family" flyer to the wall.
"What's with the cardigan, Mr. Rogers?"

I pretended my pen was a pipe. "Mental giant."

The flyer showed him, benching a million pounds.
"No, Rungers. I'll call you Mr. Rungers."

I sprayed. "I got power. Power."

He yawned and played with his weight lifting wrist
straps. "I need you to order two new Rhino benches. Get
them here by Friday. I don't want them next week. I want
them Friday. No exceptions. And make sure they got
black padding, Mr. Rungers."

I'm going to get the bastard back, for all the shit
he's given me. Like this afternoon. I was telling our
receptionist Eviana—she's Pullins' girlfriend—about
this rabbits' nest I saw in the field next to our lot. Pullins
came in and yawned. "Bunnies. That should be your
mascot, Mr. Rungers. A bunny on a cardigan. The
bunnies. Poom."

"Rabbits can outrun rhinos."

He stared at his Rhino shirt, then stretched his
slab of a neck. "Hey, power man. Evi, you know this
guy's got power?"

He won't know it, but he'll soon be immortalized on
the cover of the winter issue of Drawn by Darkness.
Everyone who reads about the dickhead protagonist in

my story, "The Tribulation of Whistler," will be reading about Pullins.

I had my lunch in the park today. There's a guy who lives next to it. He lives right on the other side of some bushes. He keeps a pit bull in a cage. He came out there, took the thing out of its cage, and then just kept whaling it across the face. The bastard.

The Tribulation of Whistler
by
Len Oster

Box in the Valley—Photography/Video Release Form

I hereby grant Beltrik Entertainment Corporation unrestricted permission to use photos and/or video footage taken of me or in which I may be included with others as part of the Box in the Valley haunted house experience, and to publish or air the same in whole or in part, in any and all media now or hereafter known, and for any purpose whatsoever for illustrations, promotion, art, editorial, advertising and trade, or any other purpose whatsoever, and to use my name therewith if Beltrik Corporation so chooses.

I have read the foregoing and fully understand the contents thereof. This release shall be binding upon me and my heirs, legal representatives, and assigns.
Signature: Jonathan Whistler s
Printed name: Jonathan Whistler s
Address: 22 Armstrong Lane s
City/state: Chicago, Illinois s

To: loster@getnet.com
From: mtowart@drawnbydark.com
Subject: The Tribulation of Whistler

Whistler's hands were freezing. He exited the restroom, then started back toward the waiting area. The voice of that oddball Curtis stopped him. "It didn't seem to be the most pressing issue."

Another voice. "It's pressing. It's real fucking pressing."

The blue rivulets that curled within the floor's concrete glowed coldly.

The unknown voice continued. "I don't want light blue."

"Periwinkle."

"Periwinkle." The man laughed. "Periwinkle feels cheap. I want quality. I don't want the typical haunted house shit. What would you expect? Orange, or black? Orange is cheap, and I don't want black. Do they even have black? Red? No. Oh, red. Boo. Blood, red is like blood. Too obvious, gimmicky. You want the last colour they'd expect. Not this cheap shit. Maybe like a brown. No, brown's the colour of shit. Listen: you take a shit, you wash your hands... and that's part of it. But copper, there you go. Fucking copper, or bronze. They have bronze liquid soap? Something that ties to all the sage and natural stuff out there? Fucking beautiful."

This was supposed to be one of the most frightening haunted house experiences in the nation, and this guy was talking about liquid soap?

The setting of "Tribulation" is important. First, Whistler and the other two guinea pigs are waiting to go into this massive concrete structure (i.e., the Box in the Valley). But all the activity takes place in the waiting area connected to the box. This waiting area is all sparse and contemporary, with glowing blue walls and these winding glowing blue rivulets in the floor. Big windows display a sage carpeted desert that leads to mountains.

Today, the pit bull owner opened the cage. The dog wagged its tail and jumped up on him. He smacked it in the face, then went into his house. Ten minutes later, he came out with an iron. When the dog jumped up, he shoved it into her stomach. She squealed and fell on her back. I could smell it. It's too much. I have to do something.

At the centre of one of the waiting room's three glowing blue walls was a dark opening. Whistler's hands felt frozen.

The woman, whose clothes fit like trash bags, gripped the first of the three seats. "I'll go first." The top of the seats attached to a roller coaster like rail that led through the opening.

There was a scent in there. Confident.

At the centre of the room, the know it all Marine investigated a beaker filled with bubbling green liquid. Then he flicked one of the red metal rabbits perched on metal poles. "Cold hands, boss?"

"A little."

"Know what that means? That means fear."

"No, it's the sink in there. Soom, that water's cold." Someday, the braggart would work at a carwash. He'd wash and wax Whistler's Vlark.

The woman touched one of the walls. "Sheh, my hands are all hot. It's all hot in here." Huge earrings. Lipstick the colour of overripe tomatoes. She was what happened when a horny truck driver, a dumb waitress, and lots of cheap beer mixed.

Sergeant Braggart took off his sweatshirt. His tank top showed arms that weren't so much muscular as bulky. "I was in Australia this one time? On this back road in the middle of nowhere. And there's these jackrabbits, just all over."

Trash Bags interrupted. "He have the heat on?"

"My girlfriend's swerving all over."

"... tell him to crank up the damn AC or something."

"I go, 'Let me drive.' I got in there and just floored it. Thump thump thump the whole way just thump thump thump."

Trash Bags opened an operable window at the base of the one glass wall, which displayed the shrub covered desert, and in the distance, a mountain range. "Wow, you're a real fuckin' hero. Can I feel your muscle?"

Sergeant Braggart smirked at Whistler. "What's with Supergirl over here?"

She pulled out a pack of cigarettes. Of course. "Lookit. See that mountain? I could climb that bastard. Easy. I climbed mountains twice that high."

Sergeant Braggart started bragging about a huge mountain that he'd climbed. Some mountain that made the one out there look like an ant hill.

The glass wall showed part of the massive concrete structure to which the opening in the other wall led. Why would this Beltrik plop a haunted house in the middle of New Mexico? And why would he choose these two nothings to join Whistler as the first to experience it? Not very business savvy.

Whistler would have called one of his underlings now. Delegated some tasks. But that weirdo Curtis confiscated his phone, and everything in his pockets. Said it was part of the experience. Whistler addressed Trash Bags. "Hey, did you go to college?"

"Yeah."

"Maybe you can tell me then? How can a person with a college education do that?"

Smoke streamed from the lips. Rotten tomatoes were easy to crush. "Sheh, you better fuckin' watch it, Mr. Vlark. Beltrik said I could."

Whistler was surprised that this lowlife, who'd likely spent most of her car time in the backseats of Chevys and Fords, recognized the symbol on his shirt.

Braggart put his hand in the green liquid. "Beltrik? You talked to him?"

She laughed out smoke. "What're you doin'? What if that shit's acid or something? Melt your hand right off."

"Like them things will melt your lungs? Where's Beltrik? You saw him? Or are we gonna have to deal with that Sally the whole day?"

The "Sally" was Curtis.

Whistler tried to see farther into the opening, but he couldn't make out a thing. He wanted to blow into his hands, or put them in his pockets.

It smelled like his Keras cologne. Two hundred and fifty bucks for that stuff. But he wasn't wearing it.

I took her. I got the pit bull. I waited until that son of a bitch was gone. There's a big iron mark on her stomach. She's wild, out of control. Strong. Eighty pounds of muscle. I have to finish "Tribulation." It's going to be tough.

I have to take this bitch to training. She's out of control. I took her running this morning. After about a half hour, she went nuts. Like she wanted to play. Kept jumping up on me, grabbing my sleeve. She ripped it. Second time that's happened. We got back to the house, and she was ready to play. So the 45 minute run was like a warm up for her.

She got into more stuff, and I showed up for work ten minutes late. As soon as I walked in, I heard the peekaboo whistle. "Sorry," I said. "I had a little issue."

"Issue? I don't understand issue. What does issue mean?" Pullins twirled the wrist wraps and rolled his eyes at Eviana, who once returned a cat because it purred too much. "What are you, slow?"

"I got a new dog. She's... a little hard to handle."

"Oh. You're dating?"

"She's a pit bull. She's powerful. All muscle. No fat." Unlike Pullins.

Pullins jerked a wrist strap. "Maybe you should fight her."

"Only weaklings fight dogs."

He grabbed one of the hundred pound dumbbells. "I need you to grab one of these. Help me take these to the weight room."

I could barely lift it. The bastard smiled. "You get that equipment yet?"

"It's coming tomorrow."

"I need that equipment."

"Tomorrow. I told them no exceptions."

He grabbed the other dumbbell. "Nice shoes, Mr. Rungers."

"Didn't have time to change them." They were my Z Peaks. Bright red. The best running shoes you can buy.

"Aren't they a little cotton candy?"

I did order the machines. I had to get red though, because black would take an extra week. Hey, he said he needed them the next week. No exceptions.

My story's gonna slay that fucker. And this bitch won't stop me. I'll take her to the shelter if I have to.

Whistler stood before the opening and made sure the others couldn't see him rubbing his hands. Inside, the wall and the seating track curved to the right, into darkness.

There was a tinkling, and Curtis, head tilted, walked with perfect posture into the waiting area. The fool's cap looked ridiculous enough. Add the glasses, the tie, and the buttoned up cardigan, and it was absurd. "My bold venturers, I'd like to thank you all for your patience. Mr. Beltrik will be with us momentaneously." The blue of his cardigan almost matched that of the walls. He addressed Sergeant Braggart. "Ah, I see you've discovered our rabbits. Have you any pets of your own, Private Leswit?"

Braggart rolled his shoulders. "Leftwich. It's Leftwich. Lance Corporal Leftwich."

"My sincerest apologies, my brave venturer. I have two dogs myself. They're such companionable creatures. Wouldn't you concur? I also volunteer at a shelter."

Whistler interrupted. "Where's Beltrik? Are we starting soon?"

Curtis tilted his head and, for the fourth time that day, applied ChapStick. "Mr. Whistler, if you'll just bear with me..."

"With the rabbits and that green stuff? This whole thing's a little bit lollipop for me."

"I imagine he'll be here within a matter of minutes."

"I'm not looking for imagination. I'm looking for reality. Reality? Are you familiar with reality?"

Trash Bags snorted and slapped her baggy pants.

Curtis pointed the lip balm at her. "The reality of the situation, my intrepid venturers, is that Mr. Beltrik will be here shortly."

The floor's blue coils seemed to make Whistler's hands colder. "He will. Okay, good. Because, you know, you took my phone, boy. And I've got people I need to stay in touch with."

Curtis capped the ChapStick, then tilted back his head. "Perhaps you're a dog owner as well, Mr. Whistler?"

"I have a pet pterodactyl. It eats dogs."

Corporal Braggart punched his palm. "And I got one of them T. rexes. Just big ass teeth and all that. And it eats fools."

"You may find it surprising that in Shakespearean plays—"

Braggart interrupted. "Nice sweater."

Curtis stretched his neck and pulled the knot on his tie. "Now if they're treated appropriately, appropriateleee... dogs can be exemplary companions. Catch my drift?"

"Sheh, you trying to say you wanna marry a dog or something?" Trash Bags' tomato lips tilted.

"Hey, let up, Supergirl." Braggart took a wide stance and raised his square chin at Curtis. "You ever go night mowing, boss? You know what night mowing is?"

Trash Bags flapped her shirt. "Jesus. We've been in here for like twenty minutes."

"Night mowing's when you go into the woods with your buddies..."

"And screw each other?"

"Let up, girl, and I'll take you to Home Depot. You can hang out with your lezzie friends."

"Oh, tough guy. I'm a big man. Look at me. I'm a big man."

"You go into the woods, right? With your night vision? And your BB gun?"

"Sheh, Beltrik getting a BJ in there or what?"

"... and gah gah gah just blow away anything that moves in there gah gah. Rodents bats dogs I don't give a shit just gah gah gah."

Again Curtis took out the ChapStick. "That seems to be a rather..." He stretched his neck. Behind him, the rabbits glimmered.

Whistler put his hands in his pockets. "Come on. Are we going to get this started or what? Beltrik... what kind of guy? I'm a potential investor here."

The green liquid continued to bubble, and Curtis pressed his lips together while, almost imperceptibly, his head quivered. "Very well, my courageous venturers. I suppose I'll get you strapped in as we await Mr. Beltrik."

This bitch—I mean that literally—is going to drive me nuts. I named her Rope; one of the first things she destroyed was my DVD of Hitchcock's *Rope*. She's ruined three shirts, two pairs of pants.

Last night? She got into five things. While I was flossing. She bit me and it punctured the skin. I sit down to write and bam! She's right there. She wants to play all the time. It's like raising a damn kid. A kid with jaws. I'm thinking about taking this bitch to the shelter.

When she bit me, she was playing, going for my sleeve.

Whistler's hands ached and his body seemed to vibrate. The gap in the wall and that scent—stronger now, like cough medicine—made it worse.

Curtis pressed a button. The three seats turned until they faced the glass wall. Trash Bags rushed to the first seat like it was a carnival beer garden.

Curtis touched her arm. "In you go."

She yanked it back. "I'm fine."

"This is your last and final opportunity to back out."

The fool would have to go before Whistler invested in the Box in the Valley. "Oh, last and final? Soom, I'm thankful and grateful that you warned us."

Curtis extended his neck and tilted his head. His bells tingled. "Now, my valiant venturers, I assure you: our actors and actresses will not touch you, so we would be greatly appreciative if you refrained from touching them."

Trash Bags pulled Curtis's tie from his cardigan. "Hey Curtis, how many chicks you fuck?"

Curtis looked at the ceiling, and his hands taloned. He tucked in the tie. "Neither the time nor the place for such inquiries." He pulled down a restraint and clasped her hands to the chair arms. Then he gestured toward the other seats. "And gentlemen, if you please."

A strand of Curtis's hair curled in front of his glasses as he secured Whistler into the third seat. He emitted a waxy scent, and the wrist clamps made Whistler's hands even colder.

Curtis pulled out a partition between each of the seats. Whistler could no longer see Braggart or Trash Bags, or the gap that led to the Box in the Valley. Just one glacial blue wall, the red rabbits, the green liquid, the desert, and the floor, which threatened like some arctic wasteland with thousands of interlacing icy rivers.

Trash Bags' voice: "Lookit. There there. A coyote. There's a coyote right out there."

Whistler only saw shrubs.

Curtis's glasses reflected blue. "We get those quite often. Now, my bold venturers, when the latches release you, we encourage you to get out and explore. You may stay together, or—"

"Sheh, I ain't staying together."

A holler came from outside. A man—he had a rifle—stumbled over some of the shrubs. "Ya fucker." He shot. Whistler felt the reverberation in his chest.

Curtis scurried to the window. "No. Don't. Please don't do that."

The man wore sloppy clothes, and what hair he had left was tousled. "Where's my soap, Curt? Bronze, I want bronze or copper or something." He ran out of view. There was another shot.

Whistler broke the silence. "Who the hell is that?"

Curtis stretched his neck. "That is the esteemed Hugh Beltrik."

A minute later, Beltrik, cigarette in mouth, strode into to the waiting area. He ignored Whistler and the others and looked toward the gap behind the seats. "There's a silver Vlark out there. Why would you get silver?"

Whistler spent fifty six thousand on that thing.

Beltrik used his hands to frame the gap. "This is great. Isn't this fuckin' great?"

"The Vlark? That's mine. I'm Jon Whistler."

"It's silver. Not sure why you would get silver."

"Soom, the 100 LB? It's a superior piece of machinery. The 100 LB."

"Silver's kind of predictable."

Who was this guy, with his stained shirt and his juvenile interior colour scheme, to criticize Whistler's tastes?

Braggart: "What kinda gun ya got there, boss? A Remy?"

"Huh? Ah I don't know. Some scoundrel gave it to me. Guy's a total scoundrel. I missed that coyote."

Trash Bags: "I could have hit that. That coyote?"

Beltrik chuckled smoke and his eyes passed over Whistler. Sneaky eyes.

Braggart: "What's with all the mad scientist stuff, boss man? That green stuff there?"

"I don't know what it means. I just like it."

This slob was nothing like the shrewd Beltrik portrayed in Lucrative Leaders. Still, he'd made millions through frightening people.

"I'm Jon Whistler. I'd shake your hand if I could."

Beltrik leaned back and spurted smoke. "It's green. It bubbles. It's fuckin' cool. Does it have to have a meaning?"

"CEO of Whistler and Ryan? We're potential investors?"

Trash Bags: "Damn, Mr. Money Man. Will you buy me a pony?"

Curtis gripped one of the poles that displayed the rabbits and held the fingers of his other hand inside his cardigan.

Beltrik swiped his phone. "What day is it?"

Whistler wiggled his fingers to get the blood flowing. "The 100 LB. Silver. What's with silver? Why not silver?"

"Aw this fuckin' asshole. God... Curt, did you send those things to Paul? The a-hole."

Whistler's Vlark cost him fifty six thousand bucks. What did this Beltrik drive? Some clown car?

Beltrik exhaled smoke before the glass wall. He pulled a thread at the bottom of his shirt. How could he wear short sleeves with the room that cold? "You look at all the horror movies, it's all the same shit: night time, monsters, concrete urban settings, sparse dark urban settings, or some dungeon space, something all torn to shit and dark. But this?" He swept his arm. "Lookit this here."

The Vlark was elegant. The Vlark was prestigious. The Vlark was Whistler.

Beltrik kept pulling the thread. "We got these freaky floor lights. We got these huge fucking windows. It's just wide open. Soap's not so great, huh Curt? And this over here? A concrete box in the middle of a wide open fucking desert? What the hell is in there? I bet you want to know. I love that shit."

Braggart said, "One time me and my buddies went to see The Long Cord, and I got this cheese? With the nachos?"

Trash Bags butted in. "Sheh, I seen The Long Cord and Scalpel Night and..."

"... there's a couple queers in front of us..."

"Curt, goddamn it, Curt." Beltrik gave up on the thread, let it hang to his knees. "There's a big ass smudge on the glass here."

Curtis gripped the rabbit pole. His hand was red.

Beltrik used his shirt to clean the window. "Forget The Long Cord and that shit. All that pop out shit. Cupboards slamming and shit popping out at you and that. Boo! I'm not talking about that torture chamber shit either."

Whistler bent his torso. Try to obscure the Vlark logo. "But those make the money."

"Prostitution makes money. Crack makes money." Beltrik leaned back and expelled smoke flourishingly. "Immersive. I want fucking immersive."

"What's with the rabbits over there, boss? You hunt rabbits or something?"

Beltrik shrugged. "They're rabbits, and they're red. Red metal. What the fuck are they doing here? I don't know. But you'll remember them. A fully immersed experience. I want to convey quality. I mean everything here. Even the soap, Curt."

Curtis's head quivered, and the ChapStick came out. "I assure you, Hugh. I will remedy—"

"That colour? That fucking light blue?" Beltrik scanned the three of them. "What did you think of that?"

Trash Bags: "It's soap. Who cares?"

"That's not fuckin' quality. That's cheap. I want to replace it with a copper colour. Something you don't see a lot. Copper, or bronze. Something like that. This is immersive. Curt, do one more seat check."

Curtis, holding the ChapStick between his fingers, shook the restraints on Whistler's seat. He dropped the tube. Whistler felt it tap his shoe.

Curtis squatted. "Mr. Whistler, allow me to apologize. There's a vestige of ChapStick on your shoe."

"Vestige? I don't understand vestige. What do you mean vestige? You'll get a clean cloth."

"I will clean it immediately." He extracted a wipe from his pocket, waved it flamboyantly.

"I don't want clean. I want spotless."

"Perhaps you'd like some chocolate truffles for your troubles? A warm hand towel, perhaps?"

Beltrik unleashed another smoke spectacle. "Silver, that thing's silver." He froze and looked out the window. "There's that bastard. Bastard." He bellowed and ran out of the waiting area.

Curtis rubbed Whistler's shoe. "Curious. I have a pair quite similar to these. Got them at Shoes for a Shoestring? Around fifty dollars, I believe?"

Impossible. Those were Keeps Executive Series, and Whistler paid four hundred bucks for them. And it wasn't at that lollipop Shoes for a Shoestring store. "Boy, dropping that stuff? Pretty foolish."

Curtis popped up, then flicked one of his bells. "You might be surprised to learn, Mr. Whistler, that in Shakespearean plays, fools are often the wisest characters."

The benches came in, blaring in red.

Pullins jerked his wrist straps. "You went to college, right?"

"Yes."

"What's your degree in? Stupid?"

"Actually, English literature."

"I don't want red. I want black."

"Wouldn't that degree more likely be in stupidity?"

Pullins leered at a guy whose ripped arms made Pullins' look like stuffed sacks. "Black, black. I said black."

"I would've had to wait another two weeks."

"What's this red? I don't want red. Not this cotton candy red shit."

I've never seen red cotton candy. "You said a Friday delivery."

"Friday delivery? What do you mean Friday delivery?"

"Friday. No exceptions."

The ripped guy scoped his triceps in the mirror. Pullins, watching, scrunched his face. "I never said that."

Pullins strode to Eviana. He stood behind her, then grabbed the arms of her chair. He growled and lifted her and she squeaked.

For the rest of the day, Pullins sat in his glass enclosed office and stared at me. I went to get a drink? He was watching. I checked out the rabbits. Bam. He was watching. I'm going to fuck him up in my story. The best thing is, he won't even know it.

Five minutes and three gunshots later, Beltrik returned. He hoisted a bloody coyote head and did a powwow dance. "HI yi yi yi yi yi HI yi yi yi yi."

Braggart joined the chant and made gunshot noises.

Curtis pulled his tie knot, then stretched his neck. "Hugh, please. This is hardly—"

"Ah Curt, ya prude." Beltrik set down the head, then looked through the circles he made with thumbs and index fingers. He mimicked Curtis. "Bold venturers, this is hardly the time nor the place. I love my dog, and I volunteer at the shelter. Do you have dogs perhaps? My bold venturers?" He laughed, and smoke spurted through his nostrils.

Curtis's face reddened. His head trembled and the bells tingled.

Blood dripped from the coyote head. The odour of Beltrik's smoke and that cough medicine scent congealed.

Beltrik tossed the head behind the seats. "Did you see this shit he got? This fuckin' soap? Hold on." He walked to the bathroom.

Curtis looked at the ceiling. The veins beneath his chin showed. "I apologize for this behaviour. He acts as if this soap issue is the end of the world."

"I smoked a few Ky-yoats. Gah gah gah." Braggart, with his backwoods pronunciation. Surely his car wasn't silver.

"Lookit this shit." Beltrik, fountaining smoke, moved the dispenser of the light blue soap in a masturbatory motion. He also held a pair of dishwashing gloves of the same colour. "This shit's not quality. I want—" He slipped on coyote blood and almost fell.

Curtis's nostrils widened. "We nearly reaped what we've sewn."

Beltrik used the gloves to smack Curtis across the face. Curtis's glasses fell. Beltrik flung the gloves at Curtis's face. "Then fucking clean it."

Curtis's bells tingled as he picked up his glasses and the gloves. The ventilation kicked in. They must have had it on way too low. No wonder Whistler's hands felt like ice. "All right, can we stop with the lollipop stuff? Can we get going with this?"

"I'll be right back, investor." Beltrik narrowed his eyes, then leaned back and erupted smoke. "The investor with the silver Vlark."

"Sheh, maybe Mr. Investor can invest in a pony for me."

Beltrik, ignoring Trash Bags' white trash comment, pretended to balance on a tightrope as he made his way back to the corridor. Did he treat all potential investors with this much contempt? Whistler should have brought his SUV. It was burnt umber. Close to bronze.

Curtis put on the gloves, then pulled out one of the red rabbit poles.

"Hey boss, be careful. Supergirl here might want her gloves back."

Curtis, clutching the pole and walking magisterially, followed Beltrik.

Trash Bags snorted. "Them gloves are yours, Mr. Army."

"Army?" Braggart laughed. "Shit no, sister. Army means 'Ain't ready for the Marines yet.' I'm a Marine."

"And you probably wear an apron too."

"... another cancer stick..."

A shout from the corridor, then clinking.

Curtis dragged Beltrik across the floor, into the waiting area.

Beltrik held the back of his head. "Curt, Curt, hold on a second Curt. What the fuck, Curt?"

Curtis crouched, then brought the hand soap nozzle to Beltrik's mouth. "Open, please."

"That stuff, cheap. That stuff what did you get that stuff for?"

"Open, I said. And down it goes." Curtis pumped the soap. Beltrik gagged and kicked.

Trash Bags' voice, frantic. "His head. What? His head is he bleeding?"

There was thumping next to Whistler. Braggart exhaled. "Boss, what's going on boss? You better let up there."

Curtis stood and used his index finger to rub his bottom lip. "You want to build these grand haunted houses, and nothing stops Hugh Beltrik, does it? So down come the trees."

Beltrik spit out soap. His head was bleeding. "These..."

"Adieux, Mr. Fox."

"These... cheap."

"My sincerest apologies, Mrs. Owl."

Curtis dragged Beltrik across coyote blood to the left of the seats, near Trash Bags. Whistler could only see Beltrik's legs.

Curtis stepped back into view, then raised his chin and titled his head.

Trash Bags' voice raised. "What the fuck? You hit him? You hit him on his head."

Curtis walked toward Beltrik and stepped out of Whistler's view. There was a grunt and a crack. The seats shook and Trash Bags screamed. Beltrik's feet squeaked against the blue coils.

Curtis stumbled back into view, then tucked a loose strand of hair back into his fool's cap. Trash Bags screamed and Braggart roared, "What? What?"

Curtis, his lips glistening, smirked at the three of them, then moved toward Beltrik again. Trash Bags screamed.

"B. Inferior. B-B-B." Curtis, his penny loafers tracking blood over the blue coils, backed into view.

Trash Bags spoke first. "Oh my god, shit. Oh my god what's wrong with you? He stomped his head. He stomped on his head."

They say people with dogs live seven years longer. Fuck that!

I tried working on my story while walking. She wouldn't have it. She kept trying to eat my notebook. If she wants something under the couch, she moves the couch. She jumps up on the table. She jumps up on the car.

If I do take her to the shelter, whoever gets her probably won't be able to handle her; they'll bring her back or worse.

I'm exhausted. She keeps me up at night. I'm only halfway through my story. I need to finish it.

There was a red bucket by the rabbits' nest today. It was filled with water, and the floating corpses of the rabbits. I confronted Pullins. He yanked his wrist straps. "Hey, the bucket's red. And red's powerful. Like you said."

Whistler, heart thumping, stared at the tattered bottoms of Beltrik's pants, and that string from his shirt. He felt a strong urge to urinate.

Curtis applied ChapStick. "I apologize for any..."

Trash Bags whimpered. "You killed him, you killed him you..."

Curtis touched his tie. "Young lady, when's the last time you said, 'I'm sorry?'"

"He's dead you killed him."

"I'd like you to say you're sorry."

"You killed him."

Curtis stepped closer to Trash Bags. The partition blocked Whistler's view. There was a rip and Trash Bags screamed. Then a snap. "Please, please just put that away... I'm sorry just please put it..."

"And off they come."

Braggart shook the seats. "What's he got? What are you doing?"

"I'm sorry no I'm sorry no no. What are you... god, god." Trash Bags whimpered.

Whistler tried to free his hands, but only managed to hurt his wrists. The blue coils glowed indifferently, and some urine slipped out.

While Trash Bags screamed, Curtis backed into view. He leaned back and placed something on his glasses. Then he danced, jester like. Nipples. They were nipples. Trash Bags' nipples on his glasses.

This bitch is too much. I don't have time to deal with this shit. Then I see her in her crate, the way her tail hammers against it when she sees me. And when I let her out, the way she flops onto her back. She twists and grunts when I rub her thighs and pet her around the iron mark.

Trash Bags sobbed and her nipples stuck on Curtis's glasses. Whistler's body felt slushy. The seats shook and Curtis's bells jingled. "Alpha. I'm the alpha. I am the alpha male."

A small stain marked Whistler's pants. Curtis wouldn't see it, but would he smell it? Would the others smell it?

The seats shook and squeaked. Braggart roared, "Let me out, boy."

"I thought I was 'boss.'"

"I'm a member of the U.S. Armed Forces."

Curtis, still tilting back his head, pointed Beltrik's rifle at Braggart. "Yes, a U.S. Marine. You've made that abundantly clear. It's rather humorous, isn't it? Aren't Marines supposed to epitomize the Western notion of heroism? Quiet and persevering and all that good stuff?"

"I'm a Marine, and if I get out of here..."

"Yet every Marine I've ever met devotes so much of his time to talking. It's rather womanly, if you think about it."

"Womanly? You're fucking womanly with that lipstick, ya fag."

Curtis approached Whistler and pulled off the nipples. "Peekaboo." He threw the nipples on the floor, then used Whistler's shirt to wipe his glasses. "Mr. Whistler, despite your overwhelming arrogance, you seem to be somewhat intelligent. Do you catch my drift about his nonstop talking?"

Blood stained the Vlark logo on Whistler's shirt. He nodded. "I don't understand... "

"Bragging about, for instance, 'night mowing.' Shooting at anything that moves? Let's give it a try, shall we?" Curtis pointed the gun downward. "Bang it goes." It exploded. Whistler couldn't stop himself from shrieking. Trash Bags sobbed.

Braggart growled, breathed heavily. "My foot. My fucking foot you fucking..." The seats shook. Blood spattered the bottoms of Whistler's pants, and the urine stain expanded slightly. He smelled a trace of it.

A pool of Beltrik's blood had crept into view. Served him right for bashing Whistler's colour selection. Beltrik and his tawdry clothing.

Curtis studied a line of blood on the blue gloves. Blood and mucus blurred his glasses. He raised one eyebrow, and addressed Braggart. "You bear a striking resemblance to this fellow who adopted a dog from the shelter."

"My foot. I'm a U.S. Marine."

"He put a dog down."

"I'm a Marine. I protect this country."

"Because it barked too much, down it went."

Trash Bags squealed. Her nipples lay among the blue coils. Whistler should have sent one of his subordinates.

Curtis pointed the rifle at Braggart. It swayed it as if it was a conductor's baton. "And I see you're a member of the Manberg Heights Hunting Club."

"How do you—"

"Let's resume our game of night mowing."

"I'm a Marine. I'm a Marine. I'm a fuckin'—"

The gun exploded.

"My hand my hand my fucking hand."

"Ah, your shooting hand? Your night mowing hand?"

Braggart roared and the seats shook and clattered.

Whistler shifted to try to conceal the stain. "Curtis, can we just please back up from this? Just for a minute?"

Curtis extended his bottom jaw and smiled slightly. "Mr. Whistler, the courageous venturer. Where is your pterodactyl, Mr. Whistler?"

"Listen. Beltrik, he's a, kind of a crude—"

"Anything that moves." The gun exploded toward Braggart.

Trash Bags whimpered and the vents clicked.

The seats did not move.

I can't concentrate. I can't fucking concentrate. She's destroyed my Z Peaks. I'm two thirds of the way there with the story. If I don't take her back, I can't finish in time.

The cough medicine scent and those nipples, lying there like demotions, nauseated Whistler. A squeak escaped his throat.

Curtis leaned on a red rabbit and stared at the bubbling green liquid. He pretended his ChapStick was a cigarette. Blood speckled the blue cardigan and gloves.

Whistler pictured exhaust stained snow lining a city street, and his bladder felt stuffed with cold quarters. "I don't know what Beltrik's deal is. Treating animals like that."

Obliviously Curtis approached him. Whistler shifted. Try to hide the stain. Trash Bags emitted a series of blubbering pleas. Typical of her gender.

Curtis leaned toward Whistler, then mimicked one of Beltrik's theatrical exhalations and released the scents of wax and cherry. "What compels you to wear a shirt like that, my bold arrogant venturer?"

To Whistler, the Vlark logo had always looked like a sceptre, or a key. Now it looked more like a lollipop. "Vlark? It's a good car."

"Let's not be foolish, Mr. Whistler. I don't think you purchased that car because you like that car."

"It's a good car."

Trash Bags screamed, "This is my body. My body."

Curtis pointed at Whistler's stain, then put two fingers on his shiny lips and chuckled. "You bought that car, Mr. Whistler, because you wanted others to see it. You wanted them to draw conclusions about you. Catch my drift?"

Whistler's cold hands shook and the glowing blue floor coils and walls stirred his queasiness.

Curtis thrust up his ChapStick. "Powerful..."

"It's high performance..."

"Wealthy..."

"Its ranking, rating, it's got a high rating..."

"Sophisticated and classy. All that good stuff?"

"But it's high performance and its rating..."

Residue from Trash Bags' nipples still clung to Curtis's glasses. "What if nobody could see your car?"

The blue pulsated in Whistler's bladder and stomach and chest. Even in his thighs. He couldn't keep his voice from quavering. "Vlark, it's a Vlark."

"What if it was just you?"

Trash Bags squealed. "This is my body, you fucker. Not yours."

"You seem to have quite an affinity for this, young lady." Curtis removed his tie, then stepped toward her and out of view. The bells jangled. "Why did you take it back?"

"What?" said Trash Bags. "Take it back? Take what back?"

"That cat. You give off the impression that you could scale any mountain, swim any sea, yet here you are. Young lady's not so strong now, is she?" He stepped out of view. "And on it goes."

"No. Don't. Please." She wheezed and the seats shook.

The bells tinkled and Curtis grunted. "Probably purred too much. Is that it? You purr too much, so back you go."

Did Curtis know about Zeus? About Whistler putting him down? Five thousand bucks, but the thing kept shitting in the condo. The wheezing and the blue lodged in Whistler's hands. The mountains stomped on his bladder. He lost control of it.

The wheezing stopped. The ventilation played with the string hanging from Beltrik's shirt. Whistler broke into sobs.

Curtis, his lips shimmering, promenaded toward him.

"I don't need a Vlark."

Curtis took a picture of the stain. "Throughout the world this will circulate."

"I don't need a Vlark."

"What happened to the intrepid venturer?"

"I was joking. Pictures, you don't have to take pictures. Please don't take pictures."

Curtis backed out of the room. "To the news channels it goes. To everyone it goes. Look at the bold venturer. Look at the all-powerful Jonathan Whistler."

The blue of the coils and the wall, and of the sky. The green liquid, the red rabbits. Whistler's body felt like cotton candy.

The bells rang and Curtis reappeared. One of his blue gloved hands twirled a cord above his head. The cord led to an iron.

As Curtis approached,

To: <u>mtowart@drawnbydark.com</u>
From: <u>loster@getnet.com</u>

Subject: The Tribulation of Whistler

Dear Mike,

Regrettably, I'm not going to make your October 1 deadline for "The Tribulation of Whistler." I'm really sorry if this screws things up for your issue.

I have a new dog, a pit bull. She's not a sit-by-your-feet, cuddle-in-your-lap kind of dog (most of the time). She's more like a jump-for-the-ball and sprint-back-and-forth-like-a-maniac kind of dog. Nevertheless, I'm starting to get her under control, but it will take some time before I'm fully there.

With her and work and running, I just can't finish the story by your deadline. Again, I apologize. Perhaps we can work something out for the next issue?

Sincerely,
Lenny

HYPERBOREAN BOOKS

THE
FOREST
GOD

by Rex Mundy

PERSPECTIVES OF THE SCORVYRN by Rab Foster

EMERYK'S PERSPECTIVE

My eyes open. I find myself looking across a surface that resembles a lake of mud. But I've never seen mud as grey and glistening as this.

Dozens of things protrude from it. Tree branches, some shaggy with leaves, others bare and poking up like fingers. A two wheeled buggy, its rear end submerged while the shafts once strapped to a horse stick into the air. A lidless wooden box with latticed sides that, with a shock, I recognise as a baby's crib. Smaller items, including a dented helmet, a broadsword whose business end has snapped off and thin, white things I suspect are bones.

Other white objects jut out of the mysterious grey mud, too broad and flat to be pieces of anything's skeleton.

I'm partly embedded in the mud myself. I hear sucking noises as I sit up and prise myself free. When I raise an arm, slimy threads dangle from it. Then another of my senses becomes operative, my sense of smell, and the stench that assails me is hideous. What am I sitting in? Decaying matter? Excrement? Or not an excretion, but a secretion?

The stench becomes too much and I vomit across the scum in front of me. By now I've stopped thinking of it as mud.

In fact, that revulsion begins to restore my powers of reasoning. I look down at what's spilled out of my mouth. Once, I understand, that'd been food I'd eaten. The amount of it suggests I'd eaten heartily too. But what, when and where had I eaten? Surely I'd dined in surroundings different from this hellish place. Had I dined with somebody else? Who—?

Who? That word is especially significant. For it occurs to me that I don't remember who I am.

I struggle onto my feet and wade towards the nearest of those flat, white objects. If I can I work out what this evil location is, perhaps my memory can trace a chain of events back from it. Perhaps I can recall how I arrived here and then solve the puzzle of my identity. I uproot the thing from the slime and lift it. It's smooth, curves slightly and has jagged edges, which suggests it's a fragment of a larger object. A large white thing that some time ago broke...

As the piece of huge eggshell drops from my hands, I raise my eyes from the surface of the mire and discover that it isn't wholly flat. At its edges, it slopes upwards and forms a ridge. I turn and see how the line of the ridge continues in a circle around me, enclosing me. I'm in the middle of a giant bowl. A giant bowl shaped nest.

Yes, this discovery sparks things in my memory. Events start to return to me. Though none of the recollections give me a shred of hope about my situation now.

FLEYK'S PERSPECTIVE

For much of the afternoon I remain in the fringes of the forest, moving among the final trees but not leaving their cover. During that time I view the Vedraks' castle from as many angles as possible. It has ramparts that stand in places and have fallen in others, so that their outline climbs and sinks like the spine of a crooked dragon. Corner towers and flanking towers rise out of those broken walls, their collapsed roofs and worn away battlements giving them the look of limbs blunted by a surgeon's amputations. But the tallest tower seems intact. In fact, it seems to have been added to. I stare at the unruly jumble on top of it, both inside its battlements and protruding over them, and identify it as a giant nest.

At last I have a sufficient idea of the castle's layout. Then I take several long breaths, listening to my chest suck in the air and expel it again. I imagine that air working its way through my lungs, replenishing me, boosting me. I think about nothing else. This is my technique when I'm about to do something of consequence, usually something that involves fighting and killing, but I sense unwelcome emotions like fear or uncertainty clouding my head. This is my way of extinguishing those emotions, so that they don't interfere with the task ahead.

For the first time ever, I do this to banish the emotion of grief.

Finally, I feel calm, ready, resolute. I leave the trees and step onto the footbridge that crosses the deep, dry trough where once there was a moat. I negotiate the many holes that yawn in the bridge's floor and pass through the entrance gate into the ruins. I go by a guardhouse, whose walls are bushy with ivy, and traverse the bailey, once gravelled but now covered in weeds that tangle around my boots.

Yet as I move towards that undamaged tower with its messy crown, my composure slips. Without warning, a thought cuts through me like a blade. Then grief cuts through me too, less like a blade than like an axe.

The thought is: that's where it took my brother last night.

EMERYK'S PERSPECTIVE

Our meeting with Harnbaal is the first memory that comes back to me. Harnbaal was someone whose infamy had spread across the kingdoms and reached even the southern frontier where my brother and I made our living as mercenaries, freebooters and smugglers.

My brother... My older brother... But for now his name eludes me.

Harnbaal lived in a precarious looking residence. Its L shaped foundations seemed too long and narrow for the two wings built on top of them, rising a half dozen storeys and ending in steep, high roofs that bristled with spindly chimneystacks. A square tower with a door in its base stood in the corner where the wings met. My brother and I approached the building in the fading light, guided our horses through a gap in the stone dyke that penned off the ground in front of it and tethered the horses to a post outside the tower. Then we struck a knocker against its door. Although I can't yet remember my brother's name, that doorknocker is clear in my memory. Its iron was moulded in the shape of a big, glowering hawk's head, with the tip of its beak the point that impacted against the timber.

A few minutes later a woman with coils of red hair unbolted and dragged back the door. She held a candelabrum with twisting stems and stalactites of hardened wax, and five candle flames fluttered in front of her. Her face had a harsh, haughty look in the candlelight, a haughtiness suggested too by the thin, sleeveless gown she was wearing, which seemed to signal her disdain for the evening's coldness.

She offered no greeting. Silently, she beckoned us in and led us up a staircase that hugged the inside of the tower's walls. At each corner where the staircase twisted from one wall to the next, there was a stand with a silver dish fixed on top. In each dish sat an egg about the size of a human head, its shell patterned with flecks and smudges of colour.

We emerged into a long chamber that'd surely been used as a kitchen once because its walls had a dozen alcoves filled with shelves and hooks. Now, instead of pots and flagons, loaves and cakes, plucked fowl and smoked fish, tubs of vegetables and baskets of fruit, it housed objects associated with sorcery. We saw potion bottles, measuring beakers, glass tubes, scales, tongs, pestles and mortars, heavy books whose bindings were an epidermal shade of pink, charts of star constellations, bones and skulls with strange symbols inscribed on them, embalmed hands that'd been neatly removed from their wrists, foetal like things in jars, small human effigies made of clay and wax. At the far end of this chamber was an arched window where a telescope sat balanced on the point of a tripod. A figure stood by the tripod, face against the telescope's eyepiece.

My brother said in a rumbling voice, "You expected us this evening, Harnbaal? We sent a message ahead of us, saying we were coming."

The woman turned from the telescope and approached us. She moved slowly and precisely on her long, thin legs, which were encased in black leggings and knee high, black leather boots. Her face was small and furtive, with faint, fine wrinkles crowding around its features. Above the face, however, her brow, then her scalp were smooth and bare. Indeed, save for a lone, black dyed pigtail hanging down the back of her black frockcoat, her head was hairless.

Exact in her movements like a bird. Bald like an egg. Those things remind me of another feature of the chamber. Against the walls between the alcoves stood glass cases containing eggs of various sizes and colours, though none had the dimensions or patterns of those mounted on the staircase.

Harnbaal looked my brother up and down, taking in his massive shoulders, his bulging arms, his sword blade with its long, tapering gleam. "Yes, Fleyk," she said softly, "I received your message."

That was his name... Fleyk.

The sorceress continued, "When my informants spoke of you, Fleyk, they claimed you were a giant. I see their descriptions weren't much exaggerated. They said you'd slain a hundred men during your exploits on the southern frontier. Is that true?"

She spoke and watched him in a slightly lascivious way, which made Fleyk uncomfortable. I judged her to be in her fifties. Fleyk was unused to the attentions of a woman so elderly. "Not a hundred, Harnbaal," he managed to reply. "But possibly not many short of it."

Then she turned and scrutinised me. "And could this gentleman be... Emeryk? To tell the truth, I'd expected someone bigger and stronger—"

That's it, Emeryk! My name!

"My brother may not look like a fighter," retorted Fleyk, "but that's no reason to doubt him. He has talents that I lack, talents that've often saved my skin. For one thing, he has brains."

She cackled, "Well, an impressive team I've summoned to my house! A fighter and a thinker! So, my young thinker, what do you think? Why have I brought you here tonight? What task do I have in store for you?"

I gestured towards the nearest of the glass cases. "I think you want us to find an egg, Harnbaal. You clearly collect them with a passion. I don't recognise all the specimens here or on the staircase, but I see ones belonging to the weben, the veng hon, the simorg and the tayango, making yours a collection from far and wide that probably cost a fortune to amass. Though people of your, um, calling are known to be intrigued by such things."

The sorceress nodded. "Obviously. The egg is nature's most potent example of magic. Life emerging from what'd been lifeless."

I continued: "So now you wish to hire us to locate another egg. And because you've chosen Fleyk for the task, I wouldn't expect the mother of this egg to be a simple crow or gull. It's a larger and fiercer creature, I'd say."

"Excellent! And where, young Emeryk, might you expect to find this egg?"

I walked towards the window, where the telescope pointed out into the darkening evening. "Wherever I've been in the kingdoms, I haven't heard of an egg laying creature that would test my brother's skill with the sword. So it must live outside the kingdoms. And it's interesting how you've positioned this telescope. It's not at an angle for viewing the stars." I looked into the eyepiece and saw the image that Harnbaal had been studying a few minutes earlier. The lenses were directed towards the northern horizon, where some mountains created a line of jagged silhouettes. From the west the sunset threw a red light across their pointed summits, so that they resembled a row of bloody daggers.

"I don't know much about this northernmost kingdom," I said as I returned from the telescope, "but I've heard rumours concerning the mountain range that stands on its outer border. I'm told the mountains are uninhabited. That surprises me because you'd expect some people to dwell there, eking out a living by cutting timber and hunting. So what keeps them away from those mountains? The fear of wolves and bears? Or could it be a fear of something else, something that flaps down from above?"

To my surprise, the red haired woman with the candelabrum spoke. She'd been such a discreet, silent presence I'd forgotten she was there. "The peasants living near the mountains claim that their slopes are stalked by something called the Scorvyrn. They say it's a monstrous, winged creature that's made a nest in the ruins of a castle there."

Harnbaal added, "Since I set up home in this region years ago, I've researched the matter. I've heard so many reports of attacks and sightings that, yes, I believe an unknown creature is at large in those mountains."

Already I was sceptical. "You say there's just one Scorvyrn. What makes you think it produces eggs?"

"Well," said Harnbaal, "some maternal instinct compelled it to build a nest. And nature gives us plenty of examples of animals, types of lizards, frogs and salamanders, that can give birth without fertilisation by a mate."

"But if that's the case, what happens to the offspring after they've hatched? Why isn't this territory overrun with the creatures now?"

"I don't know, Emeryk. Perhaps when its food stocks run low, the Scorvyrn eats its young. Being maternal doesn't necessarily mean it feels motherly love."

"Your accounts of this creature come from the peasants. Do they say anything else about it?"

Harnbaal smiled grimly. "The castle where the Scorvyrn supposedly has its nest once belonged to the rulers of a mountain clan called the Vedraks. In their day, the Vedraks had an unsavoury reputation. They were rumoured to be enthusiastic practitioners of the dark arts—"

She said this without irony. Very few items in the room around us didn't have some application for the dark arts.

"—and when the stories started about a fearsome creature nesting in the Vedraks' former home, people soon connected it with the Vedraks themselves. They reasoned that the Vedraks had summoned it into our world from hell, during one of their rituals."

"You want us to find a nest," growled Fleyk, "and remove an egg belonging to a creature so feared it's made people shun a mountain range. That's also reputed to be a demon." He shook his head. "No man can question my courage, Harnbaal, but I don't know what my chances would be fighting against an escapee from hell."

"Of course," said Harnbaal, "what I'm telling you are tales. The ignorant ravings of peasants. But listen, Fleyk. Though I'm convinced the Scorvyrn exists, I maintain it's a natural creature. A strong, fierce creature, to be sure, but strong and fierce in the manner of a lion, a tiger, a bear. In the end, it's driven by animal instincts and appetites. And as men, you have the intelligence to outwit it."

I sensed something was still being held back. "Is there anything more the peasants say?"

"They claim it can change its shape," said the red haired woman.

"What?"

"The Scorvyrn," explained Harnbaal, "feeds on flesh, sometimes human flesh. When it carries its victims back to the nest and devours them, the peasants believe it absorbs their spirit and strength... Their whole life force."

"And their form," said the red haired woman. "With each victim, it acquires the ability to take on the appearance of that victim. An ability it uses to lure subsequent victims to their deaths."

Harnbaal spoke reassuringly. "But that belief can be rationalised. As well as being associated with the dark arts, the Vedraks were warlike and observed a notorious custom after winning a battle. They'd feast on the corpses of their slain enemies. Their belief was that by eating their foes' flesh they'd also consume their life force and become stronger themselves. It's obvious that over the years the cannibalism of the Vedraks and the predations of the Scorvyrn have become confused. The legends about the Vedraks absorbing the souls of their victims have been transferred to the Scorvyrn that lives now in their castle."

None of this made Fleyk happier. "I'm trained to fight against men. But you expect me to face a creature you hardly know anything about? A creature that if I'm lucky will simply descend on me like a lion with wings? A creature that if I'm unlucky originates in hell and can change its shape to look human?"

"I understand, Fleyk," purred the sorceress. "I'm setting you an arduous task. I can only assure you that the payment for delivery of one of the Scorvyrn's eggs will be substantial." She smiled at us. "There's a vault in the east wing of this building where I store certain items of value. Let's go there and negotiate what you'll get for the completion of this assignment, shall we?"

It turned out that there were more riches in Harnbaal's vault than we'd ever dreamt of. And at the sight of that vault's contents, our misgivings about the project vanished. Winged monsters? Shape shifting demons? How could such things deter us when Harnbaal was offering us such wealth?

But now... I'd gladly give those riches to anyone who could pluck me out of this foul nest and transport me far away from it.

FLEYK'S PERSPECTIVE

Standing below the tower, among the weeds, I feel something on my face. I raise my hand and my fingers touch wet skin. I've seen other people cry, often when they're on their knees before me and pleading for mercy, but it's been so long since I cried myself that I'd forgotten the experience of it.

However, while I weep, my grief gradually changes to frustration and then to rage. To think... We'd actually begun to scoff at Harnbaal for believing that the thing existed!

Though we'd journeyed in these mountains for days, following muddy tracks through the expanses of fir and pine that covered the landscape to its highest peaks, we'd seen and heard nothing. The sky contained only drifting clouds and the occasional circling speck of a raptor. The wind carried only far off wolf howls. The derelict cottages that appeared occasionally by the sides of the tracks had caved in roofs and toppled walls but that damage seemed the result of the passing of time. There were no signs of sudden demolition, nothing to suggest that something huge had swooped down and smashed them.

By last night, our thoughts had turned to the sorceress who'd sent us on this mission. We sat on opposite sides of the campfire, eating supper, talking across the flames about what we'd seen in her vault.

"I'm even beginning to wonder," said my brother, "if she's a true practitioner of the dark arts. Maybe it's just a reputation she cultivates to keep her neighbours at a frightened distance. So that nobody discovers what she's got stored in her house."

I recalled those pieces of exquisite jewellery, works of beautifully fashioned silver, heirlooms encrusted with precious stones, crates overflowing with gold coins. "Why does she stash that treasure? Why not sell it and spend the proceeds and get some pleasure from it? Keeping it locked up seems so pointless."

"Some people are misers, Fleyk. Obsessed with hoarding wealth rather than spending it."

"And what about this mad business with eggs?"

"Rare eggs are valuable too. They're another treasure she's hoarding."

I sighed. "They seemed the only two people in the building. We should've slain the degenerate bitches on the spot." I called them 'degenerate' because it was obvious Harnbaal and her companion enjoyed an unnatural, carnal relationship. "Then we could've claimed everything in that vault for ourselves and avoided this foolish trek into the wilderness."

"They seemed alone. However, for someone who possesses such wealth, Harnbaal was very relaxed about her security. And her mansion's huge. She could have an army hidden there. But yes, I think it's time we turned back and started making plans for how to relieve the sorceress of her riches..."

Our conversation was disturbed by a troubled whinnying from the horses, tethered to a tree at the edge of the circle of firelight. I got up and walked over to them. Bandits were my concern now, since with no proper inhabitants but plenty of abandoned dwellings these mountains were probably a refuge for vagabonds from the south. I reached the horses and said soothing words to them whilst easing free the sword at my waist. I peered into the darkness beyond them, trying to discern figures—

Suddenly, I heard something in the night sky above, a flapping sound. We'd become so dismissive of Harnbaal's story that for a moment, a fatal moment, I didn't realise what was happening.

Then I did. I spun round and roared, "Emeryk, get away from the fire!"

But while he scrambled to his feet, the flames were already swirling under downward gusts of wind. An instant later, something dark and massive fell across them. I glimpsed long leathery arcs of wings and talons the size of scythe blades, and heard a squall of hellish noise, partly Emeryk screaming and partly the beast shrieking in triumph as it claimed its prey. Simultaneously the fire seemed to explode. Sparks and pieces of burning wood flew out in all directions, and I twisted around so that none of those burning fragments struck my face. By the time I'd turned back, the black monstrous thing had gone.

And so had my brother.

I stared dumfounded at the ring of scattered, burning debris from the campfire. Lying amid the debris I saw Emeryk's cloak, flames starting to eat at its edges, and the knife he usually carried beneath his tunic, which he'd had time to draw but not to use. Those two things were the only evidence that a minute earlier he'd been sitting there, talking to me.

But now I've found its abode. From the trees I saw no movement at the top of the tower, which means it's departed on another hunting trip. While it's searching for new victims, I have to find a way of climbing to that nest. And when it returns...

I don't expect to win the ensuing fight. I glimpsed enough of it last night to have an idea of its formidable size. But I can surely inflict enough pain on it to make it regret what it did to Emeryk.

Perhaps too the nest contains eggs, ones that won't ever turn up in Harnbaal's collection. The sorceress speculated that it might eat its own offspring, but I'm going to assume that within its monstrousness there's some spark of parental affection. By the time the Scorvyrn comes back today, its eggs will be fragments of shell, pools of slime and mounds of butchered flesh. That's another price it'll pay for murdering my brother.

EMERYK'S PERSPECTIVE

The amnesia has left me. I remember everything now, up to the moment when the Scorvyrn seized me.

Refusing to surrender to despair, I crawl from the centre of the mire to the slope at its edge and up that to the ridge at the top. From the ridge I find myself viewing a panorama of mountains, cloaked in coniferous forest. I lower my head. Occupying the ground directly below are the remnants of a once formidable castle. There's a dried up moat spanned by a crumbling footbridge. Within the circle of the moat, much of the castle exists only as piles of rubble and broken stumps of towers.

I realise I'm looking down from the summit of what is both the castle's highest tower and its only one to remain fully intact. The Scorvyrn chose this for its nest and packed mud, debris and probably its own dung between the battlements crowning the tower. The ring of blocks and indentations that form those battlements lie under the slope I've climbed, while before me I see that the nest's putrescence has oozed over the blocks and through the gaps to hang in mid-air in thick, dried strands.

Behind me, somewhere underneath the nest, I suppose there's an opening to a staircase that runs down the tower's interior. But I'd have to dig up the nest's miry floor to locate the opening. Of course, the simplest way to escape would be to advance a little further and drop from the ridge to the ground. But the nest's at a dizzying height. I'd have no chance of surviving the fall.

Jumping. Suicide. An option I might consider later.

I turn around, study the wreckage strewn nest again and note how some of it is concealed from view. I've assumed that I'm alone at the moment, but am I?

Could there be a living thing here that I've yet to encounter? So much detritus has been dumped in parts of the nest that something could be hiding among it.

Another question. Why am I not dead? Why did that monstrosity not kill me when it snatched me from the earth last night? Why has it delivered me here alive?

I realise that although I've found pieces of eggshell, I haven't seen a whole egg. That means there was at least one egg here but whatever was inside it is now out. Yes, it's becoming obvious that the Scorvyrn took me with no interest in eating me itself. I was intended as sustenance for the offspring that, somewhere, occupies this nest with me.

FLEYK'S PERSPECTIVE

I find a doorway at the bottom of the tower and enter. Inside, a staircase goes spiralling up the circular wall. Window slits in that wall allow beams of light to infiltrate the tower, crisscrossing the empty black shaft that rises between the coiling staircase.

I ascend, dusty beams flashing across me as I pass the window slits. At the top I emerge onto a platform where a second, narrower and steeper flight of steps climbs through an opening to the battlements. Now that opening is blocked. A mass has oozed down through it and lies over the steps, congealed and hardened, like a solidified stream of mud. I poke at it with my sword, disturbed by how it glistens, sickened by how it stinks. With time, I could reach the nest above by digging upwards through this blockage. But I don't have time.

The only other way to get there is to squeeze through the highest of the window slits, which is level with this platform, and climb the outside of the wall.

I dump my pack on the floor, remove my boots and force myself sideways through the aperture. With my chest sucked in, I manage to scrape between its sides and emerge at the external wall. I find myself perched on a lip of stone where I have a head spinning view across the ruins and forest swathed mountains. Then I turn and look up. Cracks run horizontally and vertically between the massive blocks that make up the wall. I can climb with my fingers and toes hooked into those. But if my strength fails, or if any of the cracks I'm clinging to crumble, I'll plunge and perish. And with my corpse lying broken and hidden among the weeds that cover the castle's flagstones, the creature will return and never know I was here.

I take more long breaths until I've rid myself of that thought. Then, ignoring the pain as the edges of the cracks tear slivers of flesh from my fingers and toes, I heave myself clear of the window and slowly scale the wall above me. I reach the line of jutting corbels that supports the battlements, where I have to reach outwards, find the ends of the corbels and wrestle myself up around them. At this point, I encounter the tendrils of dried filth and slime that hang from the nest, poking through the embrasures and over the merlons in the tower's fortifications. I struggle amid them with nothing but the void of air beneath me.

But my hatred for the Scorvyrn gives me energy. Like a tenacious lizard, I continue to scrabble upwards.

I make it to the ridge that covers the top of the battlements and drag myself over into the nest's putrid interior. It slopes to a circular floor and forms a basin, parts of which are cluttered with things the Scorvyrn has scavenged, such as branches, bones, even a small cart and a child's crib. I lie gasping for a time. When I've recovered my breath, I struggle to my feet and remove my sword from its sheath, the bloody ends of my fingers stinging as they touch the sword hilt. I descend into the nest and start hoisting items out of the muck to check what's underneath.

Meanwhile, I realise the air's becoming hazy and reddish as the sun drops towards the peaks of the western mountains. This impels me to search more quickly. And then I notice something else, which gives my search further impetus. In the distance, is that the flap of wings I hear?

I drag up a great branch that's still heavy with leaves and find the body of a small man beneath it. Scarlet rivulets creep away from him, unable to soak through the gel like surface of the ooze he's lying in. Much of the flesh has been ripped off him, making him unrecognisable, but the freshness of the injuries tell me he died recently.

Then, as I resign myself to the fact that I've discovered my brother's corpse, I hear a new sound, different from that of the flapping wings. It's a voice behind me. I turn with my sword raised, both hands gripping the hilt, both arms ready to swing the blade with full force.

I don't expect this sight.

Smeared with filth, a small, young man stumbles towards me. His face is both contorted with fear and glowing with hope. "Fleyk, you've come, you didn't abandon me!" he splutters. "But it's coming too! Don't you hear its wings? You have to fight it. You have to destroy it!"

Surely the mutilated corpse lying at my feet is that of my brother. Yet I'm looking at my living brother too. What's happening? Am I hallucinating? Did I lose my sanity during that desperate scramble up the tower wall? These questions assail me and I can't answer them, and the mystery so transfixes me that I hardly hear the wings any longer.

EMERYK'S PERSPECTIVE

I'd started searching the nest but the trauma of the past night and day had weakened me. Soon, exhausted, I collapsed into the mire and lost consciousness again. When I woke, the light was fading and I could hear something moving nearby. I kept still and listened, believing the Scorvyrn had returned or its offspring had emerged. Then I decided that the sounds were more like the movements of a human and I dared to raise my head and look.

Elation!

Only yards from me stood my brother Fleyk. He'd wrestled a huge branch up from the fabric of the nest and now his face seemed pained as he contemplated something below him. But at the same moment I realised we were in danger. I heard wings. The Scorvyrn was coming back.

Couldn't he hear? What was he looking at that made him oblivious to it?

Now I struggle up and shout to him. He drops the branch, raises his sword and turns towards me. His face shows recognition when he sees me, but there's bafflement in it too and the sword remains poised over his head. I stumble towards him, arms outstretched. I want to embrace him and show him that I'm living flesh and blood, not ethereal, not a ghost. Also, I need to warn him. He has to defend us against the Scorvyrn, which is about to land in the nest again.

Yet as I reach him, I hear, addressing me, a voice that doesn't belong to my brother. Nonetheless, it speaks with the authority of a senior family member.

And I suddenly understand what the food was that I'd vomited up earlier.

FLEYK'S PERSPECTIVE

It's him! Surely it's Emeryk! The corpse must be that of another unfortunate whom the Scorvyrn seized recently. It devoured him but left Emeryk to feed on later. As he staggers into my arms, however, I remember I have something else to deal with. Moments ago I heard wings beating but now the beating has stopped.

I look towards where the wings had made their noise and find myself contemplating the woman with the red hair and sleeveless gown who'd ushered us into Harnbaal's residence a week ago. How insanely out of place she looks, standing amid the nest's squalor!

She laughs at my astonishment and says, "You came here yourself, Fleyk. That's most obliging of you. I expected I'd have to carry you here as I did your brother."

"You...?" I stutter. "But... Harnbaal! This is her devilry!"

"Harnbaal? Well, she's the first human to show me some interest and respect since the Vedraks originally summoned me into this world. Also, when my offspring are sufficiently mature and independent, she kindly conducts the rituals that allow them passage back to the realm I came from. This world of yours is a wonderfully safe environment in which to raise my young, Fleyk, but its food supply is limited and it can support only one of my kind. Especially now that the mountains are empty of people and there's a limit to how far I can fly carrying a human adult.

"Indeed, that's another way Harnbaal helps me. She provides food. She recruits strong, nourishing specimens and sends them here, offering them riches in return for one of my eggs."

I scream, "You devious, shape shifting bitch—!"

Through the thickening light I see the woman become a shadow that expands monstrously. Long wings arch out from its sides, spikes sprout up from its head, the head itself swells grotesquely. Yet the woman's voice remains. "Yes, Fleyk, that's a talent of my kind. We eat, consume, acquire. Body, soul, memories become ours. Then we have the power to adopt the appearance of our prey. I've enjoyed the form of this one since the day I devoured her. I've enjoyed wearing her whenever I've had to move among your species surreptitiously and not as a predator.

"By the way, Fleyk...

"You'll observe that already my child has mastered this talent admirably."

I remember that I'm still clutching my brother. I turn my head towards him and discover that he's no longer present. Where his face had been, there's a screen of teeth. Maybe a hundred teeth altogether, arranged in two rows, those rows interlocked, each tooth as thin and sharp as a dagger blade.

And before my mind can grasp the sight of those teeth, the two rows suddenly spring apart and spring forward.

SCORVYRN'S PERSPECTIVE

Don't be confused, child. Don't be afraid. Concentrate on the meat and feed. When you've consumed this second one and absorbed his life force, it won't be so traumatic. The first one is the most difficult, because inside you there's only one spirit and one set of memories, and you can identify with those too closely. You forget what you really are. You lose sight of your own being and start to believe you are that first one.

But when you have two inside you, you'll have it in perspective. You'll appreciate that they're energies, abilities, forms you can draw on if the situation demands, but not your real self. They're appendages to your essence, but your true essence is something else.

So feed. First the thinker and now the fighter! Knowledge and strength! And before I left her mansion Harnbaal mentioned that she'd been in contact with three more mercenaries on that southern frontier. So soon we'll be welcoming another expedition into our mountains.

Searching for eggs, but arriving a little too late in the season.

HYPERBOREAN BOOKS
THE MISSIONARY DIED AT DAWN
by Rex Mundy

FROM THE AIR by Sergio Palumbo
edited by Michele Dutcher

Wearing his field service cap on his fair short hair, and a military jacket whose design wrapped over his chest and fastened off centre, secured by concealed buttons, the tall captain of the Royal Flying Corps walked in his ankle boots at a quick pace along the path.

The large training flying station he had been ordered to reach on that cold morning consisted of several metal structures, bent and curved, meant for military use—like accommodation or bomb storage. Beyond that there were three pairs of hangars, plus a single building constructed of wood and brick, not far from Farnborough Common, in England. The location was used as an emergency landing field, too. It was here, in a controlled environment, that many younger pilots from across the British Empire, including South Africa, Canada and Australia, had begun their training and gained their piloting skills during that conflict that had soon been named 'The Great War'. It was different for him; Captain Sallow had arrived at the Royal Flying Corps by chance, and had quickly become known for his growing experience. He had already been involved in many bloody air battles in Europe, especially over the skies of France, and had been aboard three different models of biplanes before being assigned to his present squadron, in the Special Forces of the Air.

The unbelievable bloodshed that such a war had exacted had changed many rules of military confrontation when compared with what warfare and combat had previously meant for a soldier. But things weren't going to improve any time soon, as they appeared to be heading downhill for the foreseeable future.

Over the course of the last few months, the military operations of the British Empire in the Middle East had consistently expanded and, unfortunately, had required many more resources than anyone had initially imagined. It had begun in November 1914, Sallow remembered, when an expedition arrived at the head of the Persian Gulf to immediately secure Britain's supplies of oil, but orders had been later given to advance further inland. There had been a false sense of security resulting from the apparently feeble Turkish resistance. But a subsequent defeat had occurred on Townshend, on November 25, 1915, and the forces were pushed to partly retreat.

On the other hand, the long range bombardment of Turkish coastal artillery batteries situated in the European part of Turkey, which had been begun on February 19, 1915 by the Anglo French battleships, in preparation of Allied landing operations, hadn't prevented the troops of the Mediterranean Expeditionary Force—including thousands of men of the Australian and New Zealand Army Corps—from remaining stuck in the place. They had suffered heavy losses. The command kept insisting—though many thought that the situation had reached the point where a decisive win against the Turkish army in that part of the country would be very difficult—that staying could only cause countless more casualties for no purpose. Not that such a war, The Great War, hadn't already caused disasters and bloody battles in many parts of the world, so far... And the increasing usage of the new Fear Gas bombs that the Germans had recently developed and launched against the British and French troops in the European battlegrounds was making things worse, causing terror in those breathing in their vapours and disrupting assault tactics in an unexpected way.

Captain Sallow, or Flight Commander as he was usually called, reached the building he had been ordered to go to that day and went inside. He was already aware that the still unknown operation he would soon be a part of wasn't going to be easy, nor something he had ever dared until that moment. The High Command was always imaginative about the ways the life of the infantrymen could be endangered, deploying them under the worst circumstances here and there, according to the commander's point of view and considerable experience, although he was only in his early thirties. He considered a new ointment designed to be applied to the skin, called Darkness's Grey, that was said to help a soldier blend into the blackness of the night and was meant to improve undetected incursions through enemy lines. However, it was also reputed to be the hidden cause of so many illnesses and deaths among the daring members of the assault units themselves…

Sallow's dark eyes, the same colour as his hair, were attentive as he sat down and focused on the hurried words of the bearded, bald Colonel standing behind the one wooden desk in the expansive room.

"Since April 24, 1915, we have received a few reports about several hundred Armenian intellectuals who were rounded up, arrested, and later executed. The Turks seem to have launched a set of measures against the Armenians, including a law authorizing the military and government to act against anyone they 'sensed' was a security threat. Some American newspapers, like The New York Times, have suggested there is a 'policy of extermination directed against them' in the Middle East."

"This seems to be a serious issue, by all means, Colonel Iltraw." Sallow nodded.

"It is, indeed, flight commander. Our sources say that it all started after the Turkish Minister of War implemented a plan to encircle and destroy the Russian Army at Sarikamish last year, in order to regain territories previously lost to Russia. Though Pasha's forces were routed in the battle and almost completely destroyed, thanks mainly to the new diesel powered armoured tanks the Russian Empire deployed in that area. Since that time, the Turkish Minister of War has publicly blamed his defeat on Armenians who, he said, had sided with the Russians in that region. This remains to be demonstrated. However, it is certain that many Armenians were ordered to turn in any weapons that they owned to the authorities and then those soldiers were either killed or worked to death."

The Colonel paused briefly, then continued. "We have also received news about executions and mass graves, and death marches of men, women and children across the Syrian desert to concentration camps with many dying along the way of exhaustion, exposure and starvation. Other details have been provided by a few western diplomats, creating widespread outrage against the Turks in the West. It seems that even some ranking German diplomats and military officers have secretly expressed bewilderment..."

Sallow stared at the other man in silence, waiting for the rest of the report that he knew was to follow.

"Newspaper articles like that of April 28, 1915, from the Atlanta Constitution, 'Massacre Continues in Turkish Armenia' or the New York Times' article from April 28, 1915—'Appeal to the Turks to Stop Massacres'—have highlighted the bloody facts that were reported, although the details appear scarce." Colonel Iltraw paused again for a few moments. "We need to know if such reports are true, or if events worse than these are in the development stages. It's the viewpoint of the higher ups that we must immediately ascertain such facts and see how the resentment, and the sentiment of revenge of that population, might be turned to the advantages of our army in our aim at defeating the Turkish Empire and gaining a decisive win in that uneasy area."

"Are we speaking of a reconnaissance flight to the Syrian desert, Colonel?" the captain asked. "This is unusual to me, and very far from the European battlegrounds."

"I haven't finished giving you all the details, flight commander. Driven forward by Turkish soldiers, many women, children, the elderly, and the infirm are presently said to be on a death march, heading into the that desert with no food and water, the marchers being subjected to periodic robbery and massacre." Colonel Iltraw spoke in an unfaltering tone. "Just one or more reconnaissance flights wouldn't be enough to make things clearer. So, you will be joining a special group and will be transported to your destination, where you'll be formally assigned, at first, to the Middle East Wing before commencing the secret operation. We can't endanger more people, and can't even let our aeroplanes land on that distant area controlled by our enemies. Is that clear, Flight Commander Sallow? This is why you'll reach the surface, not by landing, but by jumping down from the biplanes thanks to a new model of parachute…"

"Jumping down to the ground?" The inquiry exploded from the captain's lips. "Using a parachute?"

The other looked at him and, as if he had predicted and understood his perplexities, added with a smile, "Sounds strange to you, doesn't it, Flight Commander Sallow? It sounded strange to my ears as well when I first heard the details. But this is how things must be done in this case…" the older man said. "Actually, the first time I was told about the latest secret developments in the parachute project, I thought that it was an unprecedented and very modern method that might prove useful in present warfare, and to our army. The Germans were already testing it themselves, according to our agents in Europe...”

Sallow was still wide eyed.

“Then I was also told that our military would never allow our pilots to wear such a device, as the first models were reputed to be bulky, or too weighty, although the reality was that the higher ups feared that it might encourage cowardice or inspire some young pilots to escape a bloody battle in the air simply by jumping from the aircraft, to save their lives. This is sad, but it hardly will change in the following months... So, they clearly forbid our pilots from using it. On the other hand, they are asking you, or better ordering you, to jump from a considerable height into an area controlled by the Turks. This is the way it has to be. It can’t be helped, Flight Commander Sallow.”

The younger man considered it. He knew that some of the more unusual missions for pilots like him involved delivering spies behind enemy lines. There were also subsequent concealed flights to keep those behind the military front supplied with the birds that were used to send reports back to base, and this he had already done, more than once. Not all of them had made it, unfortunately, and the missions were dangerous. Now they were speaking of something entirely different, and even more uncertain, in a country far away from the European battlegrounds. This would be more bizarre than even the strangest of his unusual assignments so far.

“Two small piro-motors situated at both ends of the parachute will need to be activated after you jump and will let you choose and partly change your course, though they have a limited range of action, of course. The trainer will explain all you need to know.” Colonel

Iltraw seemed to have now completed his instructions. "One thing more: once you are in that desert, you'll be on your own. We can't provide you with horses, nor can we send any local agents with pack animals. The task would be too difficult and we have no time to prepare or deploy such resources."

What was now up to Sallow was just to nod and openly accept the orders received. However, serious doubts were rising in his mind, and even deeper fears.

"In order for us to retrieve you, allowing you to join our troops again, you'll have to get to the north western coast by yourself, from the desert area of your assignment. You will need to reach Mudanya, or Hatay... not a short journey. Hopefully, there might be alternatives... By the time you have the job done the Allied Army of the Mediterranean Expeditionary Force could have finally secured the landing base on the north western coast of Turkey and we might be in control of the damn' beaches, which is improbable at the moment. In that case, you would have a safer way to get back home."

"What if that doesn't happen and those damn' beaches are still in the hands of the enemy?" the flight commander asked the superior.

"Well, I suppose you'll have to find another escape route. There are a few alternatives, but all of them are more dangerous..."

"I see," answered Sallow, swallowing hard.

"All the other details are in the papers I'm handing to you now. I don't know if we'll meet again, flight commander. What I can do is wish you best of luck, of course." Colonel Iltraw stood up and gave the Captain a warm handshake before taking leave of him. Sallow duteously stepped out of the room. The commander breathed in the cold air outside. He knew he needed a beer after all that he had heard, though he didn't know if he could find one strong enough in a nearby pub. Maybe a stiff drink would be better, or more appropriate...

Sallow and the other six men chosen for the mission were ordered to meet next morning at a designated point in the same training facility near Farnborough Common. The flight commander was pleased that he had already worked with two of them: Hubert Maenllwyd and Edwin Roberts from the Special Forces of the Air, who were both slim, with chestnut coloured hair. The other four were: Aki Rewse as Equipment Officer, Aibne Horpe as Armament Officer, Syed Gower as Rigger, and Paul Kibler as Flight Sergeant with his strange blond, though sparse, curls.

All of them wore the formal attire that had become the official uniform of pilots of the Royal Flying Corps. Sallow still remembered when, at the start of the war, there was no formal uniform for the flyers but the military, with their wide experience of Army motor transport, had motoring garments available which they had offered to the newly formed Royal Naval Air Service and Royal Flying Corps pilots like him. So, that was how their weatherproof coats, goggles, and leather boots had come into play. After all, the Airmen needed uniforms that could protect them from the biting winds of an open cockpit while in the air. They also wore flying helmets to shield their heads and their present suits had also come into use: three layers, a thin lining of fur and an outside layer of special light material, all made into a one piece suit just like his. These overalls and goggles were regarded by pilots nowadays as the most suitable for operational use.

Airmen like Hubert Maenllwyd and Edwin Roberts, who were around Sallow's age, were well accustomed to special operations and the others were as well, as far as the flight commander knew. So his crew had some experience in many of the very unusual or perilous tasks abroad. They were all great pilots, of course.

The aeroplanes they flew were similar to the frigates from that era called Piro-frigates and were powered by steam (as well as sail). The present biplanes that pilots like them used were known as piro-biplanes as they were powered by steam as well as modern aviation fuel. By late 1915 all the aeroplanes of the Royal Flying Corps had adopted the familiar cockade markings, though contrary to usual French practice those years, they were applied to the fuselage sides as well as the wings.

The B.W.3., which stood for Blériot Working, was a refurbished French Voisin piro-biplane, powered by a 60 hp (45 kW) water cooled engine. There were a few of those in that military training facility, and the members of the mission group would be dropped from one of those aircraft during their operations in that desert abroad. Like all earlier examples of the type, the B.W.3 had parallel chord unstaggered wings with rounded ends, using wing warping for roll control, and the flight commander was well aware of those useful features. The wings were unequal in length: upper wingspan was 36 feet 7 1/2 inches and lower 34 feet 11 1/2 inches.

As the seven airmen kept walking towards the fuselage of one of those piro-biplanes, the aircraft came into full view. The rectangular section was a fabric covered wire braced structure, with the pilot seated aft, behind the wings and the reconnaissance man in front, under the centre section. This arrangement was adopted so that the aircraft could be flown 'solo' without affecting the aircraft's centre of gravity, if necessary. The main undercarriage consisted of a pair of skids: an axle carrying the wheels was bound to the skids by cords and restrained by rods. A sprung tailskid was fitted, while the wings were protected by semi-circular skids located beneath the lower wings.

Other minor modifications on the model they saw before them, Sallow noticed, included the undercarriage wheels that were moved back 12", the wings which were re rigged to have 1° dihedral, and the propeller was cut down in an attempt, to increase the engine speed.

The briefing started and all of them had to sit inside a tent where they found some chairs, a desk and the fair haired trainer, Transport Officer David Daniels, who was drawing something on a large sheet of paper situated in plain view in front of them. Next to him was the model of one of the parachutes they were meant to study and learn how to use.

"The design and construction of a parachute like this, since the beginning of our studies, is based on the thought that a chain is only as strong as its weakest link. That said, every link from the jumper to the canopy has to carry its share of the maximum load that is applied during the opening shock..." The trainer looked over the group of young but very experienced pilots who had been chosen for the difficult duty that was to be carried out in that desert area where they would be very soon deployed. At first sight, he seemed to be someone who liked to say what was on his mind without worrying about how the person on the receiving end felt hearing it. "Tensile strength is the greatest stress cloth can withstand straining along its length without rupturing, expressed as the number of pounds per square inch. The 28 foot canopy of the parachute is a polygonal structure having 28 sides, and a diameter of 28 feet plus or minus 1 inch..."

The other data and all the details about the new strange device they would be using, so as to get to the ground below from the piro-biplanes, kept coming and filled their minds, though several serious worries came with them, and left a bitter taste in all the pilots.

Daniels seemed to notice their unspoken wariness, and stared at the seated airmen, explaining, "The suspension lines are sewn into the canopy. These lines run continuously from the connective link on one side, through the canopy, and on to the connective link on the other side. The material between any two suspension lines is called a gore. There are 28 gores in a 28 foot canopy. In this peculiar type there are self inflating wings that provide control of speed and direction..." He was aware of the uncertainty, or the doubts, on the faces of the few men he was talking to, but he was from the military and just did as he was ordered. He explained what he had rehearsed over and over, spewing out what he had either been previously told, or he personally knew by experience. He had already used that device a few times during the tests he had been a part of at the base of the Royal Flying Corps Training Wing near Farnborough Common. "The parachute works, boys, I can assure you. Not perfectly all of the time, but it works. Anyway, believe me, boys, this mission will not be easy, as you well know..."

They all nodded. Paul Kibler, the flight sergeant, made a face and scratched at his sparse blond hair for a while in a characteristic way.

"Always keep in mind, boys, that opening your chute at a high speed while still low could result in a dangerous rupture of the canopy. Don't do it, at any time—just wait for your piro-biplanes to reach the required height set before jumping! Then do your best and, hopefully, in a matter of moments you'll put your feet on the ground and be prepared to do your duty." Then the trainer handed them some reference documents that offered a coverage of flight performance, overall motion, inflation management and loads prediction, other than including a detailed design example. Of course, it all had to be kept secret and couldn't be carried on their body once they were abroad in the area of operations.

Several days of hard training followed. Because the parachute was a completely new piece of equipment, they had to be used to it or they would find themselves in real trouble once in the air...

Just one week later, the group was on the move. Once the airmen reached the base in Greece where they were meant to be briefly stationed before the start of the operations, they immediately began their preparations and went through a subsequent training that had to remain completely secret. They were not even allowed to speak about the mission with the other pilots they met from time to time in the military facility or in the mess hall. Not that they saw too many people or airmen around. Their superiors did their best to keep them away from the rest of the troops, and also from other members of the Royal Flying Corps.

The day finally came and they readied themselves for their duty. As they had been told, a long high altitude flight over 18,000 feet was needed to clear the many mountain ranges on their way to the desert before they reached the jump zone. So, they put on their fur lined clothing as necessary levels of protection from the cold they would have to face, otherwise their body would give out moisture which would freeze when the high altitude was reached. Dressing had to be done in strict sequence. Underwear, close woven woollen underwear duplicating and worn loose, the two inch squared vest, inner shirt, army shirt, and so on to the Sidcot Suit provided with lamb's wool. That way, pilots could resist temperatures of minus fifty degrees C., commonly... Flight

Commander Sallow verified that all the airmen in the group dressed as needed.

What they found funny, and strange, on this occasion was that usually before the take off the pilots were clearly reminded of the fact that the clothing they wore and their equipment were the property of the public. So, any losses due to exigencies of the campaign had to be certified by the officer commanding. However, in this case it had been their superiors who had told them to destroy, or make unserviceable, the new device they would use to skydive to the ground, as no one in the military wanted the parachutes to fall into the hands of the Turkish soldiers and, by means of them, to the Germans. That secret had to be kept at all costs.

When they were in their two-seater piro-biplanes and eventually took off, their appearance didn't even look human anymore, as all that clothing, the gloves, the large goggles and the helmets on their heads would make it difficult for anyone to recognize them as such. Much as ancient knights wrapped in their bulky armour bore no resemblance to the bodily warriors underneath that wore them. Other than that, as higher altitudes meant diminished oxygen levels and increased the threat of hypoxia, they had been provided with systems for breathing made up of large masks that fitted over their nose and mouth. Though many airmen said that they openly disliked the apparent restrictions that resulted from such a weighty face covering, as reported in several air battles in Europe, and some pilots had serious problems with it, this couldn't be helped.

The long flight went well and the crew were apparently in luck as no one happened to spot them along the way, once they got past the sea, and even afterwards. In fact, they saw no one until they had almost reached the area where the piro-biplanes were to leave the seven airmen who had been brought here to jump below. Only some herders lost in the wild dusty plain seemed to notice their presence in the air, but the airmen didn't worry about them.

The desert zone now stretched as far as human eyes could see with just a few shrubs that sparsely dotted the ground. And above them, the clear sky was pale blue.

Their B.W.3 aircraft had gotten them safely to this point. Such a feat wouldn't have been possible if they had used an old oil based biplane, whose cruising range—as it has been demonstrated in several tests—was much less than this piro-biplane. There was no door to be slid open, right before they jumped. The seven men just had to get out of the cockpit by using their arms and putting their feet on the upper part of the fuselage before looking below and shouting at the pilot that they were ready. They all felt their eyes widen and their chests tighten.

Then the jump took place.

After leaving the fuselage, the men kept their feet together and their head back, looking up when they jumped. The flight commander remembered the strange sensations he had had during the first tests at the training field near Farnborough, when he was generally unable to focus on anything except how high up he was. The trainer had called it 'sensory overload'. What he and his crew had been scared of during those days at the base? Well, seriously of dying, getting wounded or losing control before touching the ground, of course. They were not afraid of heights, obviously. After all they were war pilots and had flown so many times that they were more experienced than most other airmen. This was why they had been selected for this mission. However, it was one thing to be piloting a piro-biplane, and an entirely different matter to be jumping out of it while still in the air... After so many tests, the parachutists knew that it was all mental. Words couldn't completely explain it. and yet it could be so satisfying—if you survived.

The military also reminded him of how many times he had tried to scream during the tests, only to discover that you couldn't really scream because the wind was so strong that it filled up your mouth with air. Unlike the training they had undergone in Great Britain, there were no clouds to pass by in the clear sky here, and you immediately had a 360 degree view of everything around you. Falling speed was really considerable, exactly as they had been taught, and in just ten seconds you had already covered about 1,800 ft. In a way it felt like flying.

"Make sure you always look up and down and all around during the jump," the trainer had told him. Those words resounded in Sallow's aching ears as the ground came nearer and nearer. Then the time came to activate the small ball sized attachment to release the parachute, just when his mind was getting used to the feeling of seemingly unending freefall. As expected, there was the noise of something catching the air, and the force of the parachute itself slowed him down, ripping his body towards the sky.

The flight commander imagined a time in the future when there would be many people ready to jump out of aeroplanes every day, just for a living... Who knows?

The seven men activated the two small piro-motors on both ends of every parachute that allowed for easier manoeuvrability, exactly as Colonel Iltraw had instructed that day near Farnborough. You could make it speed up and go in the direction you wanted for a longer time than any other similar fabric device, thanks to those two small rotors that let you better chose a spot to land, and you could also make the parachute rise a bit higher, or take it a bit lower. You could even increase your cruising altitude for a few minutes longer over that empty desert plain.

The right place for their landing was spotted in front of some pointed outcrops in the near distance that might prove to be dangerous, and the flight commander signalled to the others behind him to touch the ground as he was doing now, or just to follow his path the best they could. Mostly by luck, all of them noticed his gestures and did as ordered.

Once the captain and other three men touched the surface, they had to get past the after effects of the jump. The last three were still in the air and were quickly nearing the ground. One of the seven jumpers, Kibler, the flight sergeant, had to cut the ropes of his parachute and fall before it was time. The device began rotating and he fell to the desert from a considerable height, breaking his arm. The other men had seen him fighting against the device to try to make it go in the direction he wanted, but he had failed, not due to anything he had done wrongly, as they later discovered. All of his fellow flyers joined him on the plain, but they had no time at the moment to retrieve the parachute that had been cut away, as its piro-motors that had messed up kept going and took it towards the horizon. The pilots watched it disappearing into the distance.

So they had to decide what to do next and Sallow ordered them to forget about the parachute that got away. After all they were in a desert and wherever it might fall, no one, luckily, would find it for who knows how long. Anyone who knew the flight commander was well aware that he had a presence, something that made men listen to his reasoning when he spoke, even when he wasn't giving orders.

However, this was the first problem they had encountered so far and a serious deviation from the plan they had been given. Their orders were to destroy all of those parachutes once they had landed safely on the ground, but they were openly forgetting about that order. Not that they had other alternatives, anyway...

They checked their equipment, water provisions and weapons. Given their task and the many miles they had to cover in that barren dry area of operations, they had only been provided with lightweight boxes: the only materials they had were absolutely necessary and easily portable. They were well equipped with energy stimulating tonics and rousing vapours, highly recommended by the High Command for anyone suffering from fatigue, heat exhaustion or many other possible conditions during the war, according to their military manual. So, the men looked over their pistols: the pilots had been issued Webley–Fosbery Self Cocking Automatic Revolvers instead of the usual Webley MK4, which was the standard British Army Service firearm of the First World War. Though the process of opening, emptying, and loading the Webley–Fosbery was almost identical to all other contemporary Webley revolvers, it had a shorter cylinder, the overall structure was strengthened and proved to be much more reliable. It also had a speed loader to make it easier to reload the firearm, differently from a stock allowing for the revolver to be converted into a carbine. This automatic revolver was the perfect pistol for Special Forces of that time, and for this task in particular. The men also had the common British Lee Enfield 0.303 inch rifle, of course, which in experienced hands let a soldier fire twelve well aimed shots a minute.

The grounded airmen in the group studied their map and calculated where they were—or where they thought they were. Then everyone in the group put on a head cloth to protect their head and face.

"It will be a long hard journey, boys, you all know that. So, let's start walking, do our research, go back and report what we find, alive! It's as easy as that..."

"Aye, flight commander. We couldn't ask for anything easier than that... Alive, I mean." Aki Rewse, the short Equipment Officer, made his point clear.

Sallow opened his mouth in a sneer, though not too widely as he didn't want let the sand or dust in...

The warm wind brought no relief from the sun's rays. Nothing lived in the area they were moving through, and nothing could.

"With this heat, I think it would be wise for us to keep moving through the night," Aki Rewse said, following six hours of gruelling hiking in that unbearable environment.

"Unfortunately we can't stop and wait for it to come. We must keep going for a while longer, sun or no sun," Kibler, the flight sergeant, replied in a low tone. "Other than that, we must be prepared as there can be freezing temperatures in a desert land like this after sundown."

The flight commander agreed with Kibler and looked back in the direction from which they had come. He didn't say anything more, focusing instead on his new surroundings. The crew was marching over a plateau, with an altitude between 1,300 and 3,900 feet. There didn't seem to be any water ahead and he didn't see how someone could ever survive for long there. It was certainly no place for old Armenian men and women with children.

So, they all continued until they were tired and the night emerged with its brilliant stars.

"It's time to stop for today," said Aibne, the Armament Officer, a bit rumpled in his appearance because of his tiredness and the blazing heat. "We need to rest, Flight Commander Sallow."

"Yes, I agree. Set up a camp, boys. Nothing too comfortable, just whatever is necessary..." the Captain said.

So, Hubert and Edwin started preparing things and the others did their best to make camp.

As the bedding was stretched on the ground, the flight commander kept turning something over in his mind. He had experienced some unusual sensations since they had started moving through that area. Possibly, it was the strangeness of the place, or the unbelievably hot climate, he couldn't be sure. It seemed that he felt eyes on him at all times. This was why he ordered strict double guard duties as the others slept—or at least tried to.

The next morning they all woke up, started moving again, hiking all day and, in the evening, they eventually came to a spot where they found the first evidence of a mass killing.

There were corpses of young and old women, children left lifeless on the ground and, not far from those, a group of men had been shot dead. Their bodies had stayed there, under the sun, surrounded by the loneliness of those silent empty lands for, who knows, days, or weeks...? There were no weapons next to the bodies, so the conclusion was that anything useable had been taken away by the killers, or perhaps the victims had never been endowed with such things to begin with. The flight commander's second thought was probably the right one, as he couldn't imagine these old people, or the children, having weapons with them when they had been attacked.

Sallow could almost hear in his mind the gunshots, the screaming that had occurred. This was an almost overwhelming image of death, loss and destruction. Their chances of survival had been meagre to begin with, since they had been forced to walk for miles to this place where water and food were almost unattainable. It had been a very long journey for all of them before dying here. And who knows how many were still walking across that damn' desert, under the same conditions?—Probably starving... If there were others who had survived, perhaps they were still up ahead. The pilots were now undoubtedly witnesses to this genocide and they had to find them, or at least try, so they could issue a complete report about the massacre, anyway.

After taking photos, using the special equipment Syed Gower had with him, and writing rundowns about what they had stumbled into, the group continued to moving along, as quickly as they could. It was late evening when they got to a different area, with some peculiarities.

The place appeared to be very ancient ruins, or what was left of them nowadays, at the top of the mountain. The dust of the desert which was the realm of the wind, and the terribly dry climate had almost entirely reclaimed this stretch of land as their own over thousands of years of unending erosion. There was really not a lot to see among the remains of those buildings from a time long gone. The ruins appeared to be from a period before the first major civilizations of the world had come into being.

What Sallow found strange, on the ground, were the remains of many predatory birds, possibly of some Lämmergeier—it was unusual to see so many remains in a single place. At first he thought that the mass kill-off was probably a result of the harsh conditions in this desert, which was unforgiving even to such creatures that were well suited to that climate. Then he noticed something else. These remains were long birds with a wingspan of 9.3 feet, although their bony remains seemed to have been easily torn apart. By other larger creatures? Perhaps eagles? How was it possible?

As the night was quickly approaching, the captain ordered the other men to set camp, and decided the guard duties for the following hours. However, this wouldn't be a night of rest, nor would a long restful sleep be waiting for them.

All of a sudden, in the dead of the night, the two airmen watching the small extemporary camp noticed a strange noise, followed by one, then two animal calls. These calls weren't something they had ever heard before, nor were they like anything they already knew.

Then, the beat of large wings threw some powerful gusts of air to the ground and the others woke up. It was at that moment the terror began.

As soon as Sallow had risen to his feet, he looked bewildered. He wasn't sure what was happening. There was nothing in his combat experience that could have prepared him for this. How could it be? How was such thing possible...?

The monstrous flying creature—as large, and long, as two modern piro-biplanes, or more—moved across the night air like it was made of water, and its enormous wings, and legs, were just blades, streaming through the wind with unusual and apparently weightless steps. It had the wide face of a lion with an eagle head on top of the unbelievable body that was towering over them which was scarcely visible in the dark. But its appearance was something no one would ever forget, anyway.

As the flight commander breathed, his mouth stayed open as if he couldn't come to terms with the unbelievable sight he had before him, his eyes wide as he stared straight ahead.

His crewmates, too, had every reason to be terrified. Though they were excellent pilots, well trained soldiers and men who had seen almost everything, what they were now facing wasn't anything that could have been expected on any of the battlegrounds of this war.

As the captain crossed paths with the course of that winged creature, he saw just how large its mouth was: easily wide enough to eat half of his body in a single motion and skewer him like the meat of a rotting corpse. The monster unexpectedly changed its mind and headed for his fellow crewmate Paul Kibler on the left, only by chance. Before a single moment was over, the top half of the flight sergeant's body had been removed from his lower half, leaving his legs as the only remnants on the ground. Then it was the time for Syed Gower to fall lifeless to the sand.

Screams filled the night, and a few shots were fired— though the men had been previously told not to fire off their weapons in that area, as they didn't want the shots to be heard in the distance by anyone, since it might give away their location. But nothing could stop the unexpected attack. Several times the bayonets or the knives of the armed airmen were swung at the creature's head in desperate, fierce moves during the hopeless close combat. But at no time did any of their blades draw blood. Its talons, on the other hand, certainly drew blood from the two corpses from the Royal Flying Corps who had not been able to stop its attacks from the air. Each powerful blow cut either a stretch of skin on their back or along an arm. The creature moved its body in ways that the men couldn't oppose, or escape, and easily outmanoeuvred them.

It just seemed that there was nothing they could try that would make them safe. Before long the flying monster was the only one still unharmed in that place, while the bodies of Aibne, Hubert, Edwin and also Aki lay injured on the ground.

In a last attempt to fire a precise shot against the winged creature, Sallow put his hands to the large personal TL-122A flashlight he had in his equipment and pointed it towards the monstrosity to see it better.

As a matter of fact, not all the pilots in their group had packed a survival flashlight like that, and for many reasons. When the equipment had been chosen for the task it was decided that the accumulated weight of all of an airman's gear could grow to be unbearable in that desert. Also, they didn't want to overload their piro-biplanes during the long flight.

However, his move proved very efficacious, in a very unexpected way, before he had the chance to open fire, because the flight commander realised that the creature didn't like that artificial light and it moved backwards as the man pointed the device at it.

It departed as quickly as it had come. Had its hasty retreat been thanks to that light or was there some other reason? The remaining airmen weren't certain, and stayed pensive... Maybe the monster had already eaten enough for that night, or had other urges at present.

At least it had left a few of them alive.

"I think... I believe I have seen the face of that winged creature before. When the flashlight revealed how it looked, a memory came to my mind..." Hubert Maenllwyd told the others who stood around, still shaken.

"What?" the flight commander asked him. "Where?"

"A depiction of such creature was on the head of an ancient weapon my father has at home, coming from the Middle East. He found it in the desert and brought it back to England years ago..." the man maintained. "The same body, those wings, and the face of a lion with the eagle head..."

"The face of a lion with the eagle head... You're referring to some legendary sculpture of a mythological creature, I imagine..." Aibne added.

"But, I mean, how could such a creature be real?" Edwin Roberts retorted.

"You all saw it! That damn' thing killed two of our fellow airmen!" Sallow raised his voice.

"If such winged creatures do exist, they are bloody monsters..." Edwin uttered.

"Others might consider them to be fairies..." Hubert added in a low tone. "At least, this was what my father once told me about the Mesopotamian myths that were widespread in ancient times about such legendary beings. Their exact name was the Anzû, or also Imdugud. According to other versions, if I remember correctly, they were like a great bird who could breathe fire and water, the personification of the southern wind. I've seen other depictions of such monsters on a few objects coming from this region that are in British museums. Originally, it was associated with rainstorms, and its most prominent feature was its gigantic size..."

"A gigantic beast it is indeed!" an angry Aibne said.

"I always knew you were a well-educated man, Hubert," Edwin maintained. "Your family is rich, isn't it? Is this why you know so many things about ancient legends?"

"Yes, my father is a well-known academician, and took me to visit collections at the British Museum and in museums throughout the country when I was a child." The other nodded. "However, there's a lot that we don't know of these lands about things that we consider to be just legend..."

"Is there anything else that you remember which might be useful to us? So we can get out of this alive?" Sallow asked.

"I know that some old depictions of Anzû put it alongside goats... maybe goats are what it ate, or what was offered as food from the locals in the ancient times."

"I think that in this case we are the goats that monster is going to be feeding on, if we don't do something..." Aibne said worriedly.

"We're not some stupid goats. We're British soldiers, and we are armed!" Edwin retorted.

"We already saw that our shots didn't kill it: they didn't even pierce through its massive body. Maybe we missed it a few times, but even our best tries didn't have any effect..." the flight commander pointed it out. "We must find another way, and we will have to do it soon! Luckily, my flashlight proved to be of some use and made it leave... Perhaps it's a night creature that doesn't attack, or prey, under the light of the sun. If this is true, I see more trouble as soon as night comes again. But if the monster only feeds when the sun has already set, maybe we have some more time to find something to use against it..." Sallow made it clear to the others.

"But it's a damn' winged creature, flight commander! How can we kill it?" Aibne asked their Captain.

"The problem is that such beasts can fly... and those enormous wings give it enormous advantages..." Sallow noticed. Then something seemed to come to his mind, and he became really serious. "Maybe I know of a way... at least we could try this, men!"

Aibne stared at the Captain. "How are we certain that it's not going to attack us again in the morning?"

"It's possible that it has already eaten enough tonight... and I'm convinced it really hates sunlight." Sallow thought about what he had said and, looking into the eyes of his men around him, he added, "I'm sorry for being so frank, but it's just what has happened. The monster has killed and eaten two of our airmen. Actually, you know, deserts like this usually look empty but this doesn't mean they are uninhabited. During the middle part of the day, when the sun is high in the sky, animals shelter from the warm temperatures. You may see signs of them around dusk and dawn. That is when they look for food. This could be what that damn' winged creature does..."

"And what about our operations in this area...?" Edwin asked.

"Right. We must continue, those are the orders we've been given." The flight commander nodded. "However, we must bury our fellow crewmen with dignity here, bury them deep, before we move forward..."

After taking leave of the bodies of their dead, some long and hard hours of walking under the fierce sun ensued for the five airmen. Sometime after midday they spotted something in the distance, near a tall stone outcrop that seemed to have been continuously abraded by erosion caused by wind driven sand for centuries. It looked like an object they already knew, or had previously seen, though its contorted features made it difficult to figure out what it really was. There was a very old tree ahead, and it appeared to have died long ago. In its bony branches a large piece of cloth seemed to have been caught, stuck like a ripped dirty shirt on a bent hat stand. Once they approached the object they realized that it was the parachute of the dead flight sergeant!

The men were ready to take it down and destroy it, according to the rules they had to comply with during their operations in that area, but the flight commander prevented them. "I want it to be left intact, at least what it still left of it. Perhaps we can use it against that winged creature..."

"As you wish, Captain..." Aibne nodded.

"I also want you to check to see if it can be activated, just in case," Sallows added.

Hubert and Edwin did as they were ordered before making their report. "There's still fuel in its piromotors... the rotors may still work, though we don't know for how long..."

This made the flight commander think for a few moments. "Well, this is interesting. Maybe I had a good idea after all, boys..."

More hours of difficult hiking passed, worsened by the additional weight of the parachute recovered. They kept walking until late evening approached. The oncoming night not only brought cooler temperatures, but also worries about the feared image of that bloody monster that might be coming for them again.

So, the men set their bedding and tried to make preparations for whatever might be next. And it was Sallow himself who chose the first guard duty. Just as if he was expecting trouble...

By now they had a surprise for that creature if it came back!

At a certain moment, when the grip of sleep was almost having the better of the Captain, a beat of wings was heard in the air, along with a fierce call. That strange animal's call...

This was the second assault by that creature they had had to face in that damn' desert, Sallow considered. And it was at night, again... Luckily they had had time during the day to think of something to be used against it, but their chances of a win appeared to be meagre. Now that the winged monster had made it clear that it only preyed at night, they had to put into practice the strategy they had devised. It was now, or never!

Sallow awoke his fellows, then his eyes focused on the creature's moves and he believed that it was its powerful wings that let the monster manoeuvre so quickly, increasing its effectiveness. Just like the piro-biplanes they used in air warfare... Truth be told, they were humans and they didn't have wings or other means to fly in the air and fight at the height it reached. But what if they could stop its wings, or prevent the monster from making use of them so that they all could assault it on the ground? That might even the playing field.

This was exactly what they had on their mind.

"It's here! Is everyone ready?" the captain cried out.

"We need more time!" Hubert replied.

"We don't have any more time! We must try now..."

The flight commander laid the weighty rifle on his bag for better stability, then aimed and fired. The shots took the creature by surprise apparently, although the beast didn't seem to be affected by the blast, thanks to its hard skin. Hubert and Edwin opened fire, according to the plan devised to attract the monster's main attention towards them.

The creature snarled, showing its pointed teeth and thrashing its tail. Then it charged. That monstrous being wasn't going to make it easy for them to kill it.

Aibne and Aki had other duties during those minutes and, at a certain point, they signalled to their captain that they were ready. It was at that moment that the piro-motors of the recovered parachute were activated and its canopy started raising into the air, moving against the winged creature.

The flight commander stopped firing and switched on his military flashlight. He pointed it directly at the monster, hoping to get the same reaction as the previous night. The beast seemed to be affected and immediately started flying backwards. Its response was right on time, as its movements brought it near the approaching parachute that began wrapping its huge wings in it.

The monster fought against the canopy, made its wings beat harder and stronger, but it couldn't get out of the unexpected grip of that wide, resistant cloth. The creature plummeted to the ground, much to the satisfaction of the men.

But it fell too quickly...

And its huge body landed on two unfortunate crewmembers. Edwin and Aki were standing right underneath the beast wrapped up in the parachute and there was no way they could escape the impact, much to the regret of the captain.

Then Hubert threw one of the torches they had previously prepared at the monster, as soon as he lit it up. Then Aibne did the same thing.

Sallow was approaching the two to do his part and avenge the death of their fellow airmen. The downed winged creature was still wrapped in the strong grip of the parachute, whose piro-motors had stopped working by now. It was time to concentrate their efforts and hit the target many times from two sides, as the monster couldn't fly anymore. However, all of a sudden, the huge talons of the beast erupted out of a hole in the canopy that covered the monster and reached the chest of poor Hubert, causing a deadly wound. Before the flight commander and Aibne could try anything else, the fire coming from the torches previously thrown reached the small amount of fuel left in the piro-motors of the parachute and all hell broke loose.

There was a great explosion that hit Aibne, sending his corpse flying into the distance, blasting Sallow away as well.

Terrible cries followed, the crackle of the fire on the ground and then the flight commander gave out, sinking into unconsciousness.

The night went by and Sallow slept until daybreak came. As he woke and raised both his eyes to the sky, he saw that he had survived that last explosion, as incredible as it was. However, he also knew that all their gunfire, and the torches they had used the night before during that bloody battle, might have attracted the attention of the Turkish soldiers to this place—if some of the latter had been near when they were attacked.

Sad to say, what he saw in the distance appeared to be much worse than the fear, or the dangers, he had undergone the night before. It was a dusty uniformed Turkish Nefer, rifle in his hands, coming nearer. He had clearly spotted him, and others like him were approaching the point where he was now standing, seemingly waiting for the order to attack.

As Sallow looked at their angry faces, worrisome sneers appearing in their dirty beards, with large knives already covered in blood that many among them clearly displayed. He knew from just one glance that he had escaped certain death caused by that legendary creature only to be defeated in the end—at the cost of the lives of so many. How terrifying to fall into the crueller fingers of those murderers who had just left the corpses of the poor Armenian men and women they had plundered before killing. Those were fierce men at arms, who looked like man eating creatures, they had previously spared no age or sex and had mercilessly cut down young and old alike in that desert. Why should they stop as they saw some British soldier easy to take and fall into their cruel hands?

As those assassins came nearer and nearer the flight commander knew that he, unfortunately, would be their next target, the subject of their depravation and hatred. Not even his training or his courage would be enough to face the unholy torments and the bloody acts of inhumanity that were next because those beasts were undoubtedly bereft of any compassion...

PUBLISHING NEWS by Mickey Mikkelson

NEVER NEVER
Suspense at its greatest by critically acclaimed
author
Liz Butcher

*Set for release and sold through Amazon internationally
this April in eBook and Print Format!*

More than 20 years after her abduction at the hands of the elusive Pan, Wendy Darling is all grown up and a successful detective. But when a local girl vanishes in the middle of the night, her past comes rushing back.

Grieving the death of her mother, Detective Darling wants nothing more than to throw herself back into work. When the Lord Mayor's daughter, Rosalie, vanishes, she insists on taking the case, triggering memories of her own past abduction. For years, Wendy struggled with her nonsensical memories of her captor, who she only knows as Pan. Yet the more she uncovers about Rosalie's disappearance, the more Wendy is convinced her worst nightmare has come true: Pan's back. Her fears are confirmed when the girl suddenly reappears and Wendy realizes she's walked straight into Pan's trap...

Other Works by Liz Butcher:

Camille's father just inherited the family manor from his estranged uncle, forcing her to leave her friends and city life just before her senior year of high school for the small town of Woodville, England. After seeing a strange old woman lurking on the estate grounds, she embarks on a mission to uncover the history of her new home. What she finds is wilder than she could have imagined—the murder of her ancestor, Caleb LeRoux, on the same day his six-year-old daughter vanished without a trace. And an unforeseen connection to Camille herself, as the only female LeRoux born to the family in over two hundred years. With the help of her new school friends, Camille delves into the secrets of the manor, uncovering an all-encompassing truth that will change the entire course of her life—past, present, and future.

The last thing Jonah Sands expected on his thirtieth birthday was to have his life thrust into the hands of a dangerous, red haired woman—or to be the only person in the world to survive an encounter with her.

As the death toll skyrockets, Jonah and his two best friends, the siblings Tristan and Ava Carter, find themselves at the epicentre of inexplicable phenomena—a stranded ferry transforms into a barge headed for the Underworld; young girls levitate to whisper ancient riddles; technology across the globe is controlled by some unseen hand. And it all seems to lead back to the woman with red hair. When a stranger finds them in the midst of a thunder storm and offers his otherworldly assistance, Jonah finally unravels the truth about who he really is. And what it means for the rest of humanity.

Praise For Liz Butcher:

"What really sticks out from the very first chapter is just how fast the author takes readers into the action and mystery of this story." **Anthony Avina, Top Book Reviewer Book Sirens**

"Readers will love the larger-than-life characters, mayhem, and magic. I heartily recommend this book

and urge you all to grab yourselves a copy if this is your type of story. Or even if it's not!" **Reads and Reels**

"This is one impressive debut from an obviously gifted artist who knows how to blend human drama with metaphysical fantasy and mythology to create a splendidly unique novel with visceral force. Very highly recommended." **Grady Harp, Top Shelf Magazine**

About Liz:

Liz Butcher resides in Australia, with her husband, daughter, and their two cats. She's a self confessed nerd with a BA in psychology and an insatiable fascination for learning. Liz was previously the former Executive Assistant at the Horror Tree, which is a mainstream resource for authors and has published a number of short stories in anthologies including her own collection, After Dark, in 2018. Fates Fury was her debut novel and LeRoux Manor, her stunning new novel set for release, September, 2020. More information can be found about Liz at her website: https://www.lizbutcher.com.au/

"A delirious triumph of genre greatness" <http://thepeoplesmovies.com/>

"Violence has never looked so pretty"—Severed Cinema

"Glorious to behold... Blood flow like prime Lucio Fulci"—SGM

"Violent Revenge thriller that set's a new standard—Stunning"—DVDHeaven

"Stunning... A powerhouse of a film"—Twisted Minds

BEYOND FURY completes Darren Ward's very brutal and bloody crime trilogy, and is his homage to 70's/80's Italian cinema (Sudden Fury 1998, A Day of Violence

2010). BEYOND FURY was shot on a blackmagic camera in RAW 2.5K with Arri primes lenses. Production was over four years from April 2014—November 2018.

BEYOND FURY stars Italian Horror legend Giovanni Lombardo Radice (Cannibal Ferox, City of the Living Dead, House at the Edge of the Park), Dan van Husen (Spaghetti Western veteran, Band of Brothers, Nosferatu), Jeff Stewart (The Bill, Dead Man Running, Lake Placid 4), Dani Thompson, Gary Baxter, Glenn Salvage and many more.

A workprint was screened (Missing over 200 vfx and sound design) at WEEKEND OF FEAR, Germany in 2019 and Won the Silver Glibb, Audience Award for best film. The workprint was also screened at THE ROMFORD FILM FESTIVAL in 2019, it was nominated for 7 awards, winning 2 (Best supporting Actor Giovanni Lombardo Radice & Best Director).

Post production was finished March 2020 and then COVID hit... They got to the finals at the 2020 Italian Horror Fest (last 5 features out of 360). Due to play at this year's Horror On Sea festival, but again due to Covid moved to January 2022!

Darkside Releasing are releasing Beyond Fury on Blu ray April/May 2021 in North America and DigitMovies are releasing June/July in Italy. Sadly no pending UK release to report.

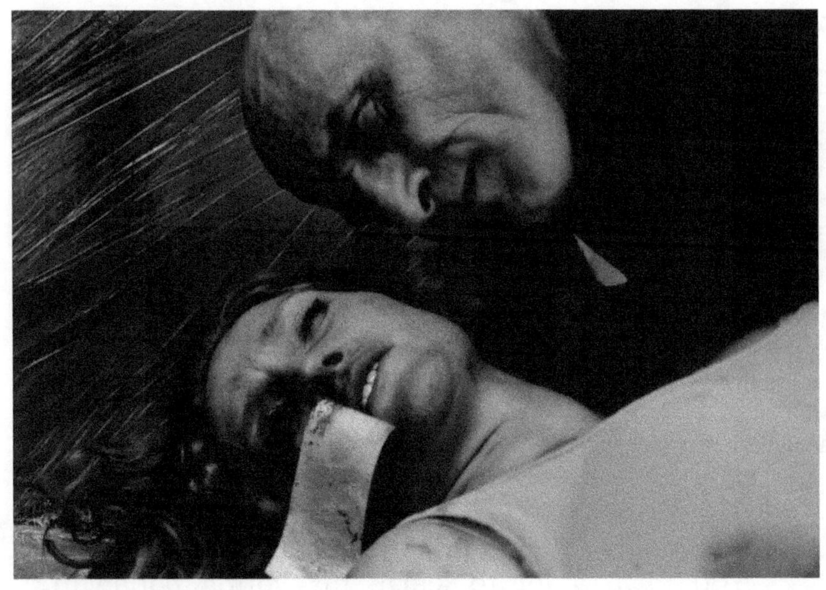

Synopsis

Michael Walker has turned his back on his Special Ops past and is about to start a family with his beautiful wife Claudia. However, a chance encounter with crime syndicate footsoldiers wipes out his future in spectacularly brutal fashion. Hell bent on ultimate revenge, Walker reawakens the savagery that earned him the moniker "Angel of Death", and unleashes an unrelenting wave of momentous violence.

Trailer
<https://youtu.be/tZQFaasHMyc>

ASSAULT ON AN OLD LADY by Christopher T
Dabrowski
translated by: Magda Woźniak

Billy loved robbing oldies going to church.

Fucking devots, they have money to fill pockets of
filthy rich priests but nothing for a man needing a
smoke!

He smoothed his outfit and ran to eighty-year-old
Euphemia. He grabbed her bag.

Frowning, Euphemia looked at him and his fingers
started to bend away. They broke from their sockets with
a crack, tore the skin and squirted blood from the stubs.

Billy was screaming.

Euphemia moved her hand. Billy bounced against
the house wall and fell down unconscious.

"You have a lot to learn, my young padawan,"
Euphemia rasped and went into the church.

Shadows Along The Road.

Josef Desade

Schlock! Publications